'When Patrick Coghlan asked if endorsement for his new novel delighted to be offered a good and accepted happily. Having r endorse this lovely book.

GW01003345

'Patrick told me the novel background theme of all thing certainly got me interested as I love horses myself. However, i didn't have to be reading long before I realised that it was much more far ranging, as it looks at what it means to have a Christian faith when facing life challenges in today's world. Its heroine, Isabel, stands in the place of all young people as she comes face to face with wounds from her past, deep rejection issues and fears for her future. Themes of relationships, bullying, life choices, hope, care and forgiveness are woven into this very believable and interesting story. There are plenty of humorous and poignant moments too. I think it is a great book for teenagers and young people and has a "rooted in reality" message of hope that is so desperately needed today.

'Well done, Patrick, for this great new novel.'
Tracy Williamson, Author and Speaker, MBM Trust

'An engaging book of faith, trust, and resilience for the seeming impossibilities that arise while involved with horses. The plot majors on bullying and the vulnerable and proves a test case for relationships as acceptance, kindness, sacrifice, justice and forgiveness surely come to the fore as a vital witness to the ways of faith.

'Set within the unique and rich context of a busy equestrian centre, it shows that prayer is a comfortable conversation with God and that His plans are far more wondrous than we could imagine. This an absorbing read, offering a unique understanding of a young woman's motivating faith as she walks through life's challenges and sees provision and transformation.

'An ideal book to feed the faith of young readers in a relevant and enlivening way.'
Sandie Shirley, journalist and author

Crazy About Horses

Patrick Coghlan

instant
apostle

First published in Great Britain in 2022

Instant Apostle
104 The Drive
Rickmansworth
Herts
WD3 4DU

British Library Cataloguing-in-Publication Data

A catalogue record for this book is available from the British Library.

This book and all other Instant Apostle books are available from Instant Apostle:

Website: www.instantapostle.com

Email: info@instantapostle.com

ISBN 978-1-912726-56-1

Printed in Great Britain.

One

February

Isabel waded through thick black mud as she approached the dilapidated wooden field gate. Each step she took rendered a loud squelching noise as she fought to keep possession of her favourite Wellington boots – the ones covered with multi-coloured polka dots, with a fluffy lining. A stale, earthy smell filled her nostrils as she struggled further to untie the knotted bailer twine that secured the gate – in her gloved hands.

Isabel looked up at the black storm clouds and mumbled disappointedly, 'Looks like more rain to come.'

She felt a shiver go down her back as she glanced at her phone and sighed. It was only 3pm and yet it was almost dark. She pulled her collar up, so she could feel the comfort of its warmth close around her neck. It triggered a flashback to her early childhood, to her mother's words before sending her off to school on winter mornings: 'You need to keep your collar up. It will keep the cold out!' She pictured her mother's kind eyes and warm smile as she used to wave her off to school from the front garden. But the close mother–daughter relationship didn't last, and now Isabel missed that closeness more than words could express.

In response to a rustling sound, Isabel glanced behind her. There was nothing there, except for the hilly landscape, bleak in its winter clothing. The heath seemed to be so lifeless, dotted with gaunt, leafless trees; each of them leaning over, distorted, as a result of years of torment from biting coastal winds.

Isabel turned round and cupped her hands together: 'Diana!'

There was a loud neigh in the distance, and then the dull thud of galloping hooves fast approaching. Isabel looked across the meadow in front of her, towards the salt marshes of the north Norfolk coastline. The flatness was only interrupted by the occasional ancient church, the remains of a windmill, a scattering of flint dwellings and barns, and a few solitary trees and bushes.

A very pretty 16.1hh skewbald horse came into view.

'Come on, girl. Look at you. Your rug is filthy – you've been rolling again.'

Gently putting a leather headcollar onto the elegant head of the young, three-quarter-thoroughbred mare, Isabel prepared to return her treasured friend back to a warm stable. The horse nuzzled Isabel's shoulder affectionately, and then snorted loudly.

'Let's get you home.'

Moments later, they approached the purpose-built stable yard, adjoining a 300-year-old white, rendered, thatched farmhouse. It was a curious mixture of ancient and modern. Heads popped over the stable doors as other horses looked out to investigate the sound of clattering metal shoes advancing on the concrete path outside. They began to call to each other, excitedly.

Isabel led the mare into her clean stable, breathing in the scent of fresh shavings. She could feel the warmth from the horses next door. Isabel tied up the mare, and then sighed again as she stretched her aching muscles. She had never imagined that her childhood dream to work with horses – recently come to fruition after leaving school at the age of eighteen – would be such hard work or such long hours… and very cold at times! But despite that, she smiled; she was so crazy about horses!

She threw her hands up into the air. 'Thank You, God, for enabling me to work with horses!'

'Isabel!' a familiar voice called from across the yard. It was her employer and friend, Karen.

'Over here!' Isabel popped her head out over the door, removing her woollen hat. She brushed her dark hair back from her face with her hand. 'Oh, I hate my hair; it's like a bunch of dangly, coiled-up springs.'

'I have to speak to you.'

Isabel sensed anxiety in Karen's voice as the young woman approached without her usual self-confidence. She was clutching a large, brown envelope.

'What is it? What's wrong?' Isabel asked. 'That envelope looks very official.'

Karen shook her head. 'I can't tell you here; let's go into the house.'

After quickly changing the mare's rugs and removing the headcollar, Isabel nervously followed Karen into the farmhouse kitchen. There was a lingering aroma of burned toast. She stooped to miss the low beams, and then sat down at the large oak table, near the kitchen range. Isabel smiled anxiously at Ben, Karen's husband, sitting in the old wooden armchair, eating a chocolate bar.

'I don't know where you put it all,' she remarked, always envious that, despite eating a diet that seemed to consist mainly of cake, chocolate and sugary fizzy drinks, he never seemed to put on any weight.

He popped the last piece of chocolate into his mouth, then leaned forward. 'Has she told you yet, Isabel?'

'Told me what?'

Karen took a deep breath as she slowly removed the letter from the envelope. She studied the contents of the thick, gold-embossed notepaper for a moment, peering through her small, metallic-framed glasses, before beginning to read it out, slowly and clearly.

'It is with deep regret that I write to inform you...'

At that moment, the door flew open.

'Karen, you need to come quickly. I think Henry has got colic.'

Alec, a young groom who had recently joined the yard as an apprentice from the local equestrian college, was nervously fiddling with the door handle, looking paler than usual. Henry was a rather valuable 17hh chestnut Hanoverian stallion that belonged to Karen.

'I'll go out right away. We'll have to speak later, Isabel.'

Karen bustled out of the house, followed closely by Isabel. By the time they reached the stable, Henry was in considerable discomfort. Karen was in tears so, not wasting any time, Isabel pulled out her phone to call James Monroe, the vet.

'Be there as soon as I can,' he promised. 'Remove any food from the stable, keep an eye on the horse and make sure he doesn't roll about and get cast or hurt himself. Under these circumstances, it is not uncommon for horses to get wedged in the stable, while they are rolling. You could try quietly walking him around the yard for a few minutes.'

It was a very tense half-hour as they waited for Mr Monroe to arrive, especially as walking Henry around didn't seem to be helping. The two friends were all too aware of the possibly serious, and even life-threatening, effects of some forms of colic and the resulting issues.

'It never rains, but it pours,' Karen mumbled, shivering. 'What with this, and the letter.'

Isabel put her arm affectionately around her friend. 'What's it all about?'

'I can't tell you now; we'll speak later.'

At long last, a black 4x4 swerved into the yard, lights blazing, and a man in his mid-fifties jumped out. He grabbed his bag from the back seat and hurried over, standing head and shoulders above the two girls.

'It's no worse,' Karen said with forced optimism. 'I walked him around, but it didn't help.'

'I'll go in and examine him,' Mr Monroe replied.

Isabel grabbed a headcollar. 'I'll put this on and hold him while you examine him,' she volunteered. 'He can be a bit grumpy.'

Moments later the experienced equine vet emerged from the stable, followed by Isabel. He frowned as he took a deep breath.

'How is he?' Karen asked anxiously.

'I need to go to my car,' Mr Monroe replied. 'I am going to have to use a stomach tube to get some fluids into him. There seems to be a blockage.'

It was not a process that the horse enjoyed. He snorted and threw his head up angrily as the vet and his two assistants grappled to try to get the tube in place, via one of his nostrils.

It was ten o'clock that night before Henry began to settle, much to everyone's relief.

Isabel went to her room in the rambling old farmhouse and fell into bed, exhausted, too tired to even think about what was in the mysterious letter.

Two

It was Isabel's turn to do the early morning feeds. She didn't mind: she had always been an early riser, and enjoyed watching the horses hungrily chasing the food around their feed bins with their prehensile lips. Henry was just having a bran mash after his attack of colic, according to Karen's instructions. Isabel poured boiling water over the bran, mixing it carefully with a large wooden spoon. It smelled better than it would probably taste, she thought – at least for a human.

'Not too wet,' Isabel mumbled, as she put a cloth over the top of the bucket to let the bran mash steam.

Alec came running in, looking half asleep. 'Sorry I'm late!'

'No worries.' Isabel understood; she had a younger brother who wasn't a morning person either. 'Would you take these feeds out to the front row, please?'

He yawned. 'Have you seen anything of Karen this morning?'

Isabel shook her head. 'I hope everything is all right.'

'Shouldn't it be?'

Using her discretion, Isabel made the excuse, 'She was really worried about Henry having colic last night. You know how much she thinks of him.'

The young groom nodded. 'I'll take these feeds out, then.' He grinned as he spotted the bran mash. 'Our lecturer at college wouldn't agree with using that.'

'I'll call you when it's ready,' Isabel replied. 'The old remedies can still be the best!'

Henry was a lot better; he didn't seem to think much of receiving nothing more than a bran mash for his breakfast. He was used to a large, high-protein feed; after all, he was a competition horse and should be having a selection of mares to be put in foal in a few weeks' time.

Just as Isabel was clearing up the feed shed, she heard the back door of the house bang shut. She looked out just in time to see Karen hurrying across the yard, looking tense and anxious.

'Have you been crying?'

'Just a bit worried about Henry – you know!'

'He's fine now. You know that! What is it really? What's that letter all about?'

'Come over for breakfast in five minutes, we can talk then.' Karen called out to Alec, 'Breakfast in about half an hour! I need to talk to Isabel, confidentially.'

As Karen walked back towards the house, Alec spoke to Isabel. 'Sounds ominous… What's that all about, do you suppose?'

Isabel shrugged her shoulders. 'I can't imagine! But one thing is for sure… I'm soon going to find out.'

Isabel made sure that Basil, the stable cat, wasn't asleep on one of the feed bags before she shut the feed shed door securely. Then she hurried across to the house.

As Isabel walked into the farmhouse kitchen, there was a wonderful smell of bacon, egg, sausage, beans and freshly brewed coffee.

'Come and sit down,' Karen greeted her.

'Breakfast smells good, what are we celebrating?' Then Isabel thought better of what she had said. 'Sorry, that just slipped out.'

Karen brought two plates of food to the table. 'Help yourself to coffee.'

'Did Ben get away OK this morning? I know he had an early start.'

'Business meeting in London,' Karen nodded. 'I'll come straight to the point.' She reached across to the dresser for the letter that she had started to read out on the previous day. She began, *It is with deep regret that I write to inform you of the sudden death of my client, Mr Richard Brooks.'*

'Who's Richard Brooks?'

'He owns all this,' Karen pointed out of the window. 'Well, he did: the house, the stable yard, the meadows… everything!' Sudden tears glistened in her eyes. She poured some coffee, and continued. 'The gist of the letter is that we have the option to buy, otherwise the whole place will be going up for auction on 15th August – with vacant possession.'

Isabel found she couldn't speak. All of a sudden, she wasn't hungry. She realised that 'with vacant possession' meant that they would all have to move out – horses and all!

'It's a long day ahead; I suppose we should try to eat something,' Karen said.

'How much do they want for this place?'

Karen sighed deeply. 'More than we can afford. Market value, I expect. We've got just over six months to raise well over £500,000.'

Not a good start to the day, Isabel thought, grimly.

The following day was another early start for Isabel. It was Sunday morning, and that meant one thing.

'It's church today!' she announced to Basil – not that he was bothered, as long as he had his breakfast. Isabel leaned forward with a cup full of cat biscuits, which she placed carefully into his well-worn dish. 'Now, don't gobble them down all at once and make yourself sick,' she told him.

By the time Karen and Alec arrived at the yard, Isabel had almost finished doing the feeds.

'Whatever time did you start work today, Isabel? It must have been at the crack of dawn!' Alec commented. 'Too early for me!'

'She's going God-bothering this morning,' Karen quipped.

'What?' Alec looked confused for a moment, until the penny dropped. 'Oh, you mean church?'

'That's not a very nice thing to say, Karen. I thought you were my friend!' Isabel smiled, in the knowledge that it was just meant as harmless banter; still, it hurt. It reminded her of the critical way her mother used to speak about her faith.

'It's a joke. You need to learn to laugh at yourself.'

'Didn't sound very funny to me,' Alec commented.

Karen gave him a look of disapproval, so he hurried off to start mucking out the stables.

'Well, since you're going to church, Isabel, perhaps you could say a prayer about the situation here. We certainly need it. Not that it will make any difference,' Karen added, sceptically.

Ben had arrived, clasping a mug of steaming coffee. 'There's nothing to lose if she says a prayer, is there?'

'You concentrate on getting your caffeine fix,' Karen retorted, a little sharply.

Isabel tidied up the feed shed, feeling quite irritated by the comments that had been made, even if no malice was intended. She wanted to bang the lids down on the feed bins. She wanted people to hear that the comments crossed the line of respect and kindness. But she didn't... she wouldn't!

'I'm not one to bear a grudge,' Isabel said to herself, as she walked up the road later that morning. 'And I suppose I can forgive them for what just happened.'

Isabel recalled the night she decided that Jesus was real and she wanted to follow Him, almost eight years earlier. She remembered her grandmother talking about how God forgives so we need to forgive too. It had been such a comfort at the time, after feeling she had been in the wrong so often, coming to the realisation that she could actually be forgiven; but since then, it had also become quite a challenge, because she felt an obligation to be forgiving towards others – people who had upset or hurt her in some way. 'I suppose I've got to go on forgiving my work colleagues when they mock me for being a Christian – again and again!'

> *Hi, God. I'm feeling irritated… and maybe a little cross. Is it OK to get cross? Sorry if it's not! Please help me not to hold a grudge against the people I work with, when they make fun of me for going to church and for spending time in prayer. It's sometimes difficult to forgive!*

She paused thoughtfully.

> *But I'm sure You know just how I feel! I know they probably don't mean any harm… but it's hurtful. It brings back memories of my mum's harsh criticism when I was growing up. Still, they weren't to know, I suppose. I know You like to help us, so I'll leave it with You to deal with in the way that You think best. Amen.*

That morning, Will, the minister at church, talked about the Old Testament story of David and Goliath.

'Goliath was a really big guy. He loved confrontation, and was a bully,' Will told the congregation, before picking up a plastic sword and shield, posing as a mighty warrior. 'Goliath challenged someone to face him in combat – anyone! But everyone was afraid. Everyone except for this young lad who looked after sheep. He was called David. He believed God would win the victory for him; and He did.' Pausing for a second, the young minister concluded, 'God can win the victory for us.'

God can win the victory? Isabel sat up. She figured that maybe God could sort out the situation at the equestrian centre for them and decided to begin to pray regularly about it – starting from now. She'd told Karen and Ben she'd pray. So she did.

At lunchtime in the farmhouse, Isabel could feel tension left over from the conversation earlier that day. She felt awkward as she sat down at the table.

Ben, obviously trying to be friendly, started up a conversation. 'Did you once say that you've been riding horses all your life, Isabel?'

Karen banged a large dish of mashed potato and another of cabbage onto the kitchen table, before sitting down with the instruction, 'Help yourselves.'

Ben ignored his wife's terseness and repeated his question. 'Did you start riding horses when you were a really small child?'

'I was only four years old when I started riding a tiny Shetland pony,' Alec interjected, fumbling with his fork and dropping it onto the floor, 'twelve years ago.'

Ben and Isabel exchanged smiles.

'No, I didn't ride horses when I was little,' Isabel replied. 'I've been riding for about five years now.' She lowered her eyes, suddenly. 'It was my lovely grandmother who took me to the stables, when I stayed with her in Lincolnshire – she was so generous. She died about a year ago and left me some money, with the instruction that I should use it to buy myself a horse and pay for its keep, until I could afford to fund it myself.'

'Your grandmother sounds very special,' Ben commented.

'She was. I miss her so much. She was my constant support. And she always believed in me. She would have been so proud of me working with horses now; unlike...'

'Unlike?'

'My dad was happy for me to do any job that I chose, as long it was to become a lawyer! He used to say, "That's the kind of job our sort of people do" – whoever "our sort of people" might be.'

'That's rough,' Alec commented. 'My parents were just happy for me to get a job and bring some money into the household.'

'My brother wants to do a law degree at Oxford so he's been the favoured one for some time now,' Isabel added.

Alec winked at her and passed the potatoes.

Over pudding, Karen examined the programme for the afternoon. 'I've got a lesson to take at two. Perhaps you two could get the beds and hay nets ready for tonight?'

Isabel looked at her employer, as if she were waiting for something.

'Please!' Karen's face broke into a smile.

Isabel grinned. 'Of course we will.'

It was a cold, overcast afternoon when the three grooms bundled out of the back door. Isabel was desperately trying to pull on another coat.

'However many layers have you got on this afternoon?' Alec said, as he rubbed his hands together, trying to warm them up.

'I've got an extra jumper, a waistcoat and a quilted jacket.' Isabel paused before adding, 'At least, I will have, just as soon as I can get the jacket on.'

They hurried into the tack room and all three came out equipped with a grooming kit in one hand, a bridle over the shoulder on the same side and a saddle over the opposite arm.

In unison, they called, 'Back!'

Three horses and ponies moved away from their stable doors simultaneously, allowing a groom in to prepare them for their rider.

Once Karen's lesson was underway, Alec and Isabel started filling up hay nets, clad in dust masks. It was quite hard and dusty work, shaking up the hay and squeezing it into the nets.

'The nets never seem to be quite big enough,' Isabel remarked.

Alec hooked the hay net he was filling on to the little spring balance hanging from the ceiling. 'It needs another kilo in it,' he moaned. 'It's no wonder we're so strong – forcing so much hay into these little nets!'

'I wish!' Isabel squeezed another large handful of hay into the net she was filling. 'Only another twelve nets after these two.'

'So, is working with horses all that you hoped it would be, Isabel?'

She grinned. 'Absolutely!'

'Even with the cold, the mud, the long hours, the dust and the hard physical work?'

Isabel nodded. 'Even with... whatever you said.'

Alec put his ear near to the door of the hay shed, obviously listening to make sure that Karen was still teaching in the outdoor school, before he mischievously whispered, 'Even when Karen is having an off day?'

'Even when...' Isabel paused, and laughed. 'Of course, even when Karen is having an off day.'

'Come on; we need to get these hay nets done: we've still got to remove the droppings from the beds, fill the water buckets, tie up the hay nets, feed the horses and sweep the path.'

Later in the afternoon, when the lesson had finished, the horses and ponies were all put away for the night and Isabel had finished feeding and was just tidying up the feed shed, Karen swung open the door and came in.

'Well done for getting the yard sorted out for the night – thank you.' Karen seemed uncomfortable as she hovered there.

'That's OK,' Isabel replied, as she made sure all the feed bins were shut.

'I... er...'

'Yes?'

'Well, I just wanted to say that I didn't mean to upset you this morning.'

Moments later, Alec popped in, as Karen hurried away across the yard.

Isabel shook her head and smiled. 'I think Karen just apologised to me.'

That night, Isabel went to bed thinking about everything that had happened and wondering what the next few months had in store for the stables – and for her, in her first year of working with horses.

> *Hi God. I know You've got a good plan for my life. I believe horses are part of that plan. And I really believed that this was the right job, too… So, I'm beginning to struggle to understand how it's all going to pan out, with that letter… Amen.*

Three

A cloud of depression seemed to be hanging over the whole equestrian centre. The recent news from Richard Brooks' solicitors appeared to have squeezed the last drop of enjoyment out of every daily activity. Even exercising the horses across the heath first thing in the morning seemed to have become a bit of a chore. Isabel no longer felt the same awe and wonder from seeing the frost-covered cobwebs twinkling in the sun, or from being out in the bracing morning air.

Back in the kitchen, Karen and Isabel were able to experience the comforting warmth from the range as they sat at the kitchen table.

'There must be something we can do to raise the money,' Isabel reasoned. The girls had just returned from a 'fun' hack and Ben was grabbing a coffee, dressed in his business suit, ready to go in to work.

'Oh yes, I think I've probably got more than £500,000 in my piggy bank upstairs,' Karen replied sarcastically.

'I suppose we could try to win the lottery...' Ben suggested. Karen rolled her eyes. 'Or perhaps not!' He leaned back against the table. 'Of course, there's always your wealthy aunt.'

Karen looked at him, sharply.

'Perhaps she'd like to invest some money in a working stud farm and equestrian centre,' Ben said. 'That's all.'

'Yes, and she'd probably want to move in with us, and... well, you know what she's like!'

Ben shrugged his shoulders. 'Sorry! Only trying to help.'

'I know you are.' Karen got up and gave her husband a hug.

There was a long silence, before Isabel commented, 'We could try to find an investor – not necessarily your aunt! – to buy the property and rent it to us; or we could find somewhere else that's suitable.'

Karen sniffed, trying to hold back the tears.

'I want to be able to make things OK,' Ben said, helplessly, 'but I don't know how to. This is one situation that can't be put right with a bunch of red roses or a box of expensive chocolates.' He finished his coffee and Isabel noticed the irony of his 'I'm the boss!' mug. 'I need to go.'

As Karen began collecting the mugs from the large oak table, she concluded, 'Or we could just sell up all the horses and close down!'

The back door creaked open. 'Am I too late for a coffee?'

Karen glanced round from putting the mugs into the old butler sink.

'I'm late!' Ben, carrying a black leather attaché case, brushed past Alec, in a hurry to get to work.

'Sit down, Alec, and I'll put the kettle on,' Isabel volunteered.

Though he could probably sense the ongoing tension, Alec made no comment. Isabel allowed herself a little smile. She, like Ben, didn't like confrontation or disagreement of any kind.

Soon after lunch, Karen was giving Henry some gentle exercise in the outdoor schooling area. After his enforced rest following his bout of colic, he had come out of the stable in a particularly lively frame of mind. He was a big, strong, slightly wilful horse at the best of times, and did not take kindly to periods of inactivity. Karen struggled to keep him in a quiet trot, as the Hanoverian stallion persisted in trying to break into a canter.

Isabel strolled over, after watching from a distance. 'Feeling any better now, Karen?'

Her employer brought the big horse to a reluctant halt. The sweat dripping from his neck and loins indicated his level of stress. 'I just feel so disappointed. I've put everything into building up the school. Henry is just beginning to make a name for himself in the competition world. I've got some mares lined up to be covered by him in the spring…'

'Working somewhere like this has been my dream as well, and I've only been here for a few months. That's why we can't just give up!' Isabel bit her lip. 'Ben's only trying to help, you know.'

Suddenly, Henry threw his head up into the air and stamped his hind leg, anxious to get going again.

'Steady, boy!'

As Karen prepared to get back to work, Isabel called out, 'So what are you going to do?'

'I need to get Henry back to work before he catches a chill.'

'But what are you going to do about the yard?'

Karen didn't look at her. 'I really don't know.'

With that, she rode off.

It was soon after that the phone rang in the centre's office.

Alec rushed to answer it, with Isabel close behind. 'Hello, Henry's Stud and Equestrian Centre, can I…' Alec handed the phone over to Isabel. 'It's Ben. He's asking for Karen.'

'Hello, Isabel speaking. Karen's not here at the moment.'

'I can't believe what's just happened. It almost seems too convenient, you know?'

'What? Don't keep me in suspense.'

'I've only got us a potential investor.'

'Really? That's amazing. How…'

'He just walked into the office, interested in making some financial investments, and said that he was in property.'

'I can't believe it!' Isabel took a deep breath. 'Maybe that prayer is working already.'

'Tell Karen he's going to follow me home to have dinner with us tonight. He wants to see the place.' Ben paused. 'Well, as much as he can, under the floodlights.'

'OK, I'll tell Karen to put in an extra helping of potatoes.'

The call ended and Alec demanded, 'What's that all about?'

'Um…' Isabel hesitated, wondering what to say. 'I expect you'll find out later.'

There was a new sense of optimism as clients arrived for the 3pm lesson, which Isabel was taking. The horses and ponies were standing in the stables, already tacked up, when everyone arrived. Roger: a grey gelding with a hogged mane that was beginning to grow out and looked more like a well-worn toothbrush. Albert: an elderly, 16.1hh bay thoroughbred gelding who had spent three years of his life racing – not particularly successfully. Molly: a big Irish draught-type horse. Derek: a 15.2hh black gelding. Cyril: a very stocky 14:2hh black and white cob gelding, who looked as if he would be better suited pulling a cart. Maria: a quiet 14:2hh chestnut Arab cross mare. Dotty: a 13.2hh chestnut Welsh mare. Flash: a 13hh bay gelding. And Max: an aged 12:2hh grey gelding.

'If you'd like to get your horses and ponies out and then you can mount up in the outdoor school,' Isabel instructed.

She loved teaching people to ride. She was always very humble about her ability as a horsewoman, although she had great hopes for herself and Diana as they prepared to enter the local competition circuit – and they were showing great potential.

Three-quarters of an hour later, as Isabel called the ride into the middle of the school to draw the lesson to a close, her heart sank as she was once again struck by the realisation that things might not work out with their potential investor. The days of the centre could still be numbered.

'Be positive…' she told herself under her breath. 'Everything will be resolved this evening.'

Karen, Isabel and Alec – who had now been told everything that was going on – made a special effort as they prepared dinner together: beef stew, Norfolk dumplings and assorted vegetables, followed by apple pie and custard.

'Here they come!' Isabel called out as she spotted two sets of headlights coming into the yard.

'You'd better stop staring out of the window and let them in, then,' Karen said, and smiled.

Isabel put a hand on her friend's shoulder. 'It's going to be all right – you'll see!'

The door opened and Ben came in, followed by a man who looked to be in his fifties, who marched in, full of self-confidence.

'This is Desmond Crawford-Smith,' Ben said.

'Pleased to meet you.' Karen shook their guest's hand.

Alec and Isabel just smiled at him.

As Mr Crawford-Smith removed his coat, he revealed an expensive-looking pinstriped three-piece suit and a blue tie. His red face seemed to be fixed in a permanent frown. Isabel felt intimidated by the air of power he seemed to radiate, but she was determined to think the best of him.

As Karen took his coat, the aroma of mothballs wafted around the kitchen. 'Do come into the dining room and sit down, Mr Crawford-Smith – or shall I call you Desmond?'

He strode across the dining room carpet, his leather shoes creaking with each step he took. 'I can't abide familiarity.'

'Mr Crawford-Smith it is, then,' Ben winked at the girls.

The chair creaked loudly as their visitor sat down.

Dinner was interesting. It turned out that their visitor lived in Sussex and was up in Norfolk looking for investments. He had accumulated a large amount of money through business deals.

After demonstrating a very hearty appetite, Mr Crawford-Smith suddenly stood up and called everyone to order as he announced, 'Time to have a look round. I'll lead the way!'

Isabel was taken aback by his forthrightness.

Karen hurried after him towards the back door, handing him his coat on the way. 'I'll put the floodlights on in the yard and outdoor school, so you can see something of the grounds and outbuildings.'

'You'll have to come back in daylight for a better look,' Ben said.

'I certainly will. You can be assured of that!'

'Nice car,' Alec whispered to Isabel. 'Must have cost a fortune!'

Mr Crawford-Smith seemed to be fascinated as he looked around the extent of the grounds – as best as he could see them under the artificial lighting. He appeared particularly interested when Karen pointed out that there were also twenty acres of meadows.

After he had seen round the outside, he glanced at his watch.

'Is that the time? I must be going, got some emails to send when I get back to the hotel.'

'But,' Karen began, 'you haven't looked around the inside of the house yet.'

Mr Crawford-Smith shrugged his shoulders. 'I'll glance around it when I come again. I need to come in the daylight for a better look at the extent of the grounds.'

As his very expensive-looking car purred gently out of the drive, there was a long silence, which was eventually broken by Ben.

'I couldn't help noticing his intense interest in the land, but none at all in the house or the facilities,' he commented. 'Seemed a bit strange, don't you think? I would have expected him to have shown a bit more interest in the bricks and mortar, and the rental value of his potential investment.'

'I didn't like his manner,' Isabel added. 'Some of his business deals seemed rather dubious.'

'It's unusual for you not to like someone,' Karen commented. 'You usually see the good in everyone.'

'He could be our new landlord,' Ben pointed out.

'Perhaps we should start looking around the local estate agents for an alternative site. And I'll contact Aunty Florence in Cambridge – it's worth a try,' Karen added, to everyone's surprise.

The next day passed quietly. Karen seemed to be feeling more positive about things, which helped to keep up the general morale. Henry was settling down into a routine once again, which made life easier.

'I think I'm going to see if I can get local sponsorship for Henry,' Karen suggested to Isabel. 'After all, he is doing quite well with his jumping and dressage.'

Isabel was a little concerned that when he started covering mares in the spring, he might not be quite so focused on his schooling and competition work, but she didn't want to knock her friend down when she was in a better mood. 'Well, it's worth a try.'

'Perhaps the local saddlery… or even somewhere like an estate agent or factory?' Karen looked thoughtful. 'And maybe I'll invite my aunt to come and visit.'

It was later in the evening that the centre's phone rang. Isabel was quick to answer it. She heard the familiar voice of Mr Crawford-Smith. 'Hello, Mr Crawford-Smith, what can I do for you?'

'Which girl are you?' he asked bluntly.

'This is Isabel speaking.'

He grunted. 'I'll speak to you and you can pass on what I say to the rest of your motley crew.' There was a short pause. 'I am phoning to say that I was very impressed by the redevelopment potential of your equestrian centre site. I don't need to come and look at it again; I have made up my mind… I shall be putting in an offer immediately, followed by a planning application – so get your bags packed, quickly.'

'What!' Isabel exclaimed. 'The idea was for you to buy the land and buildings and rent them to us.'

'Change of plan, young lady.'

With that, the line went dead.

Isabel felt her face turn pale. Mr Crawford-Smith wanted to turn them out to redevelop the site! He was putting in an offer straight away! How would the others react to that news?

That night, Isabel prayed.

Hi God. It's me again. Sorry to be a bother... but I know You never see it that way – You're always really pleased to hear from me. I wish my dad and mum were! But this isn't about them... I'm going to do some moaning tonight, though. I really thought Desmond Crawford-Smith was going to be our answer to prayer: that he would buy the whole property and rent it to us for an affordable amount. But now he tells us that he wants us out, and is going to clear the site for redevelopment. What's happened to Karen's and my dream? I thought the dream was from You. But I know that You know best and have a good plan. Please help me to accept Your will – whatever that might be.

Thank You for your unconditional love for me, and all Your goodness.

I'll speak again tomorrow. Amen.

Four

At breakfast the following morning, Karen appeared to be beside herself with worry. She banged the marmalade jar down onto the large wooden kitchen table. 'That's it, then! We'll have to close.'

'There must be something we can do,' Isabel said.

'It's at times like this that I really miss my parents,' Karen told her, wiping her eyes with a tissue. 'Dad was always so wise in a crisis. He would have known what to do. If only they'd stayed at home, not taken that plane...'

'I'm so sorry, but we can't just sit back and lose the centre. Shall we give the solicitors a ring, to find out where we stand? And then...'

'You ring them if you want to. I can't talk to them right now.' Karen shook her head. 'The letter with all the contact details in it is on the desk in the study – you can't miss it.'

Moments later Isabel returned to the kitchen grasping the envelope in her hand. 'It's probably best if I go to speak to them in person,' she reasoned. 'The office is just outside Norwich. But I'll give them a ring first to book an appointment. Could you have a word with them to say that you're happy for me to speak to them about the situation?'

Karen nodded. 'OK. You can take the car; the keys are by the house phone. Thanks for doing that. I'm... *struggling* a bit at the moment.'

After making the phone call, Isabel went upstairs to change out of her working clothes into something appropriately smart, including her treasured gold cross and chain that her parents had given to her – when their relationship had been better.

Having been driving for only a matter of months, Isabel was excited to be taking her friend's bright red hatchback – although she felt the weight of the responsibility of her mission on her young shoulders. The drive was mainly cross country, often slowed down by getting stuck behind large sugar beet lorries or other farm traffic. But despite that, less than an hour and a half later Isabel was sitting in the car outside the solicitor's office. She shortlisted the questions she needed to ask and glanced into the rear-view mirror to see if her hair was tidy, before going in.

A young receptionist sat at a small desk in the corner of the entrance hall, surrounded by telephones and computer screens. She appeared to be so preoccupied with filing her nails that she didn't see Isabel come in.

Isabel coughed, loudly. 'I've got an appointment to see Mr Sumbuso – Isabel Price.'

'Please take a seat. I'll let him know you are here.'

Isabel sat down in the corner of the waiting area, in an orange plastic chair, next to a pile of out-of-date magazines and a redundant coffee machine. She watched as the receptionist phoned through to the solicitor before continuing with her manicure. Isabel feared that the future of the centre was largely dependent on what information she could glean from this visit.

Moments later, a smart gentleman came out of one of the offices. 'Ms Price, please come through.' He indicated for Isabel to sit down in front of a large, leather-clad mahogany desk. Certainly this office spoke more of affluence than the shabby reception area. As Mr Sumbuso picked through the mountain of files and papers that were leaning precariously on top of a nearby shelf, he smiled politely. 'I'm sure I have Mr Brooks' file here somewhere.'

Eventually he found it and, letting out a large sigh, said, a little condescendingly, 'I understand that you are here under the authority of your employer? What can I do for you?'

Isabel took out her list and glanced at it. 'Well,' she replied. 'I have been led to believe that a property developer is interested in buying Henry's Stud and Equestrian Centre to redevelop the site.'

Mr Sumbuso looked a little surprised as he prised a large paperclip from the top left-hand corner of the papers in the dark-brown cardboard file. 'I see, Ms Price.' He hesitated. 'I was not aware of that.'

'As you can understand, we are all very concerned about the possibility of ending up on the street, together with all the horses, at a moment's notice.'

'"We",' the solicitor paused, 'meaning yourself and your employer?'

'That's right, and everyone else who lives at and is involved with the centre.'

Mr Sumbuso put on his small, metal spectacles and began to rummage about further in Mr Brooks' file. 'Terrible situation,' he commented. 'Mr Brooks wasn't very old – who would have expected it?'

'It certainly came as a shock to us,' Isabel replied.

'I'm sure it did… I'm sure it did. We none of us know what lies ahead, do we?' Mr Sumbuso suddenly and victoriously held a sheet of paper in the air. 'Here it is!'

'Is that something important?'

'Just wait one moment, young lady.' The solicitor read all the small print before announcing, 'As I thought. You have until 15th August this year to raise the money to buy the centre. If you fail, then the property will go to auction, with vacant possession. You will have twenty-eight days after that to move out. Until the auction, no one else can buy the property away from you.'

Isabel leaned forward in her chair. 'Are you absolutely sure that no one but my employer and her husband can buy it prior to the auction?'

'Yes. Completely!'

'What if we can find a financial backer before then?'

'That would be fine under the terms of this bequest; someone else can buy it on your behalf and then come to whatever agreement for rent or repayment, but no one can buy it without your agreement until the auction.'

Isabel was so relieved. 'Thank you so much, Mr Sumbuso. Now all we have to do is to get the money somehow.'

Mr Sumbuso raised his eyebrows. 'I expect it will be a considerable sum that you will need to raise in a very short period of time.'

'Yes,' Isabel replied. 'I expect so. Thank you for your time.'

As she was driving towards the coast, she felt some relief that Mr Crawford-Smith could not buy the property before the day of the auction. However, there was still the problem of raising more than £500,000 before that date – no mean task. Isabel shivered; it had turned colder; the temperature was barely above freezing. She turned the car heater on to full and redirected the vents. It was nice to feel the warm air rushing out on to her face.

She could see that the sky was turning grey and cloudy.

'Looks like it could be a storm,' she sighed. 'More rain – more mud!'

Isabel switched the radio on and began to sing exuberantly to the music. She swept her hair back from her face and smiled to herself, feeling quietly positive. 'If only I could help Karen to feel more positive about the future! Oh, here comes the sleet,' she groaned, as there was a sudden deluge.

Isabel turned on the dipped headlights and flicked the wipers on to full speed. They struggled to keep the screen clear. She slowed down, trying to see the road ahead. The sleet was hitting the ground with such force that it was rebounding several centimetres off the surface. Water was beginning to accumulate at the sides of the country lanes, as the drains were still full from the already wet season. Isabel was beginning to feel a bit nervous. She slowed the car down to a crawl and turned on the air conditioning, in an effort to clear the condensation from the windscreen. Glancing in her mirror, she could see two headlights behind, approaching quickly.

'Going a bit fast for these weather conditions,' she muttered to herself.

Soon, the car was hovering close behind, pulling in and out, apparently considering whether or not to overtake. This served to increase Isabel's nervousness. In an effort to comfort herself she mumbled, 'Not too far to go now. Through the woods and then I'm nearly back.'

Isabel put her foot down, speeding up a little, trying to increase the space between her and the car behind. She glanced in her mirror for a moment, feeling quite intimidated by the driver's apparent impatience, and then back to the road ahead. The sleet wasn't easing, and everywhere seemed to be getting darker, not only with the weather, but also with the shade produced by the large oak and beech trees.

She felt uneasy going at the speed at which she was travelling, but the driver behind was pushing her to go faster all the time. Muttering a short prayer for God's protection under the circumstances, she glanced in the mirror again. As he tailgated her, she could see the face of the young man driving the car. She looked back to the road and braked for the sharp corner, just before leaving the woods. The tyres screeched as she accelerated out of the bend. Then, suddenly, without any warning, a small muntjac scurried across the road in front of her.

Instinctively she stamped on the brake, and the tyres squealed again as the car swerved out of control. It all happened so quickly: one moment the car was on the road, the next it was flying over the bank into a field.

The next thing that Isabel was aware of was being in an ambulance, with the siren blaring, and intense pain in her right leg.

'It's OK, dear, you're on your way to hospital. Try not to move too much; you've been in a nasty accident.'

The paramedic was a kindly woman, with short, bleached hair – evident by the dark roots. The male voice of the ambulance driver suddenly called through.

'Is everything OK in there?'

The paramedic replied, 'You concentrate on your driving and I'll look after the patient.'

'I remember a deer; and a car close behind,' Isabel recalled, 'but nothing is clear.'

'Don't worry about that at the moment.'

'Was the man in the car behind OK?'

The paramedic looked confused. 'Get some rest. We're nearly at the hospital now.'

'But there was a young man in a car, tailgating me.'

The paramedic frowned. 'There was no one else involved. You hit a deer and the car left the road. A passing motorist – a local woman – called for the ambulance. She stayed with you until we arrived.'

The pain in her leg was getting worse. Isabel reached down.

'It's OK dear; we've put something on to your leg to support it. You'll probably be in plaster for some time.'

At the hospital, as Isabel waited for an X-ray, a kindly nurse spoke to her.

'Can we telephone someone for you? Parents or your partner?'

'My parents have moved to France,' Isabel replied, sadly. 'And I'm not with anyone. You could call Karen, my friend, please.'

A couple of days – and an operation – later, Isabel was sitting in the day room, with a full-length plaster cast on her leg, reading a magazine about horses. She was in considerable pain and discomfort, and feeling even less glamorous than usual. She longed to have a bath and wash her hair... even if it would make it frizzier than ever!

'I thought I told you to keep your leg up on the stool,' a nurse reprimanded her as she popped her head around the door. 'You need to do it to try to keep the swelling down.'

Isabel sighed. 'It's so uncomfortable sitting like that.'

'Are you in any pain?'

Isabel nodded.

'I'll see if I can get you something to help.'

At that moment, an older man with his arm in plaster shuffled into the room in a large pair of brown cord slippers; he was wearing a dark-green towelling dressing gown. 'Mind if I make a phone call in here?'

'Be my guest.'

Isabel noticed that the gentleman had a kind face. He had obviously been quite handsome in his younger years, but now his greying hair was receding, the laughter lines were spreading and his stomach was giving in to the pull of gravity. She placed him at about sixty-five.

'Stan,' he said.

'Sorry?'

'My name's Stan. I'm in here for a broken arm.' He held up his plaster cast, and smiled. 'Sorry, you've already guessed that, I expect.' Stan shuffled across the room. 'I have to phone my elderly neighbour, Roy. He depends on me so much. His son... well, I can't remember when his son last came to visit his dad.'

'That's sad,' Isabel commented. 'But I'm sure he appreciates your support.'

'Well, I do my best.' Stan got the number up on his phone. 'I came in here because I didn't want to disturb people in the ward – some of them are sleeping.'

'My name's Isabel, by the way.'

'I'm pleased to meet you, Isabel.'

He sat down on a stool in the corner. 'Roy... It's Stan. How are you?' Isabel sensed concern in his voice. 'Don't worry, I'll be home soon and then I'll help you to fill in the form.'

Isabel gazed around the little room. It had obviously been redecorated recently in a minimalist style. There was a large print of an unusually stacked pile of cobblestones hanging on one wall, and a selection of mismatched easy chairs, footstools and tables adorned the floor.

Isabel turned back to her magazine. She turned the page to see a large, full-colour photograph of a very pretty skewbald gelding. She had always liked skewbald horses – she believed that she was rebelling against those in the horsy world who frowned upon 'coloured horses', the skewbalds and piebalds. Isabel put it down to prejudice; probably because historically many coloured horses lacked quality – but things were different now.

She was miles away, thinking about her own beloved horse, Diana, when suddenly Stan spoke to her again.

'Poor old Roy; he received a form in the post and now he's worried sick. I always help him to fill in the wretched things.'

Isabel smiled. 'Forms can be so complicated, can't they?'

Stan's eyes focused on her magazine. 'Isn't he beautiful? Reminds me of a little brown and white pony I rode as a child – William.' He smiled. 'I love skewbald horses and ponies. I used to dream that one day I would set up a stud farm and only breed skewbalds.'

Isabel burst out laughing. 'Ditto!'

With that, a long conversation developed about Henry's Stud and Equestrian Centre and, of course, Diana.

Playfully, Isabel blurted out, 'You're not rich, are you?' Then she felt embarrassed. 'Sorry, I was only kidding.'

Stan shook his head. 'I'm afraid not.'

'Ah, well! Anyway, you must come and visit.'

At that moment Karen barged in, carrying a newspaper, a large bunch of slightly overripe purple grapes and a box of chocolates.

Before Karen had even really greeted her friend, she said, 'Isabel! We were all so worried about you.'

'I'm OK. Really. Could have been a lot worse. Thank God.'

'Thank God? Why didn't He protect you from that car accident?'

Detecting the genuine fear in her friend's voice, Isabel replied, quietly, 'I could have been killed, but I wasn't!'

'I suppose. But now how are we going to manage, with you here in hospital, in a plaster cast – and with my car written off?'

'Stan, this is Karen. Karen, this is Stan. He's a horse lover as well.'

Karen appeared irritated. 'I'm glad that you can disregard it just like that. Wait till I tell you what has happened on top of all this. I really don't know what to do next!' She held up the newspaper and read:

> *Yesterday, property developer Mr Desmond Crawford-Smith revealed plans for a large holiday development to be built on the north Norfolk coastline. He told our reporter, 'I stop at nothing when I have seen a development site that I want.' When asked if he had found such a site for his holiday development, he declined to reply.*

Isabel drew a deep breath, 'I see what you mean.'

Stan looked on. 'You really have got problems if he's interested in developing your place.'

Karen looked annoyed that this apparent outsider was intervening in their private business, but despite that, she continued. 'I can't understand why Ben didn't know what that Smith man was like. I blame him for all this!'

Isabel decided to take charge of the situation. 'I'm sorry that I'm going to be out of action at the centre. I'm mortified about your car getting written off. And I wish that Crawford-

Smith didn't want to redevelop the site. But it's no good blaming anyone. What we need to do is to find solutions to our problems.'

Karen went quiet; she looked slightly embarrassed. 'I'm sorry. I just can't stop thinking about losing the centre.'

Five

March

'What are you doing?' Isabel quizzed as she swung herself across the kitchen floor on her crutches, and sat down heavily on the old wooden armchair at the head of the table.

'I'm writing a letter. What does it look like?' Karen replied sharply.

Isabel was beginning to get very tired of Karen's attitude. 'It's not easy for any of us, you know. And to crown it all, believe it or not, I'm in a lot of pain today.'

Karen pressed down the space bar of her laptop with great force. 'You're in a lot of pain! What about my car? My pride and joy – or had you forgotten about that? I have to drive about in this awful little lime-green loan car for weeks until the claim and everything is sorted out. How do you think my car is feeling, all bashed up and with the roof cut off, in the scrapyard?'

Isabel began to smile.

'Do you find this funny?'

'Not really. It's just… your car… like it was a person.'

Karen burst out laughing. 'I suppose I should be grateful to your God that you survived with no more than a broken leg – despite being knocked unconscious.'

'He could be your God as well.'

Karen ignored the comment. 'I'll put the kettle on for some tea.' She filled the kettle at the old butler sink and placed it carefully onto the range. 'Have you contacted your parents yet?'

'Why should I want to do that?'

'About the accident, silly – they should be told.'

Isabel frowned. 'You know how it is. They don't contact me, and I don't contact them.'

Karen got the mugs down from the dresser. 'You can have the "I'm the boss" mug today.'

Isabel smiled.

'But seriously. You should sort this thing out with your parents. I wish mine were still alive.'

'OK, I'll contact Mum if you contact your rich aunt – is that a deal?'

'Who do you think this letter is for? I'm writing to Aunty Florence. Perhaps she can use some of her millions of pounds to help us out. After all, she's got hardly any other relations apart from me – well, maybe that's an exaggeration. I'm inviting her to come up to stay with us for a pre-spring holiday, by the bracing north Norfolk coast.'

Isabel grinned. 'I think you're doing the right thing. She'll probably be only too pleased to help out her favourite niece in a time of economic crisis.'

Karen laughed and shook her head. 'It was never like that, I assure you. We didn't really hit it off. You wait until you meet her!'

Isabel had arranged a lift into town to do some shopping. 'If you let me have the letter, when you've finished writing it, I'll get it posted for you – assuming you don't have an email address for your aunt.'

'You assume right!' Karen replied, as she clicked on 'print'.

Isabel found it quite a struggle sliding in and out of the back of the car with her plaster cast. She wondered if she would manage OK with walking around town, still being quite a novice on crutches. So what was intended to be a relaxing morning out began with Isabel feeling a little tense, not only about coping with the broken leg but also with concerns about the equestrian centre and what the future held. She dreamed of an envelope falling onto the doormat, opening it up and discovering a cheque from an anonymous benefactor that would solve their financial crisis... but this was real life, not a fairy story!

She clasped the letter to Aunty Florence in her hand as she went into the post office for a first class stamp – it seemed to be their only hope at the present time. As usual, the queue looped from side to side and almost as far as the door, and there was a cold breeze every time it was opened. She looked across to the counter and sighed. A large woman, with long, greying hair tucked back into a ponytail, had stacked at least twenty-five brown paper packages neatly near the scales. Each one had to be weighed individually. Further down the counter, another member of staff was preoccupied with checking a large bag of loose change and, at the same time, carrying on a conversation with a gentleman in a charcoal-grey suit.

'Come on,' Isabel mumbled, irritated.

'In for a long wait,' the young woman in front of her commented.

A small elderly man a little further forward in the queue looked at his watch. Obviously late for an appointment, he pushed his way to the door and scurried out. Isabel followed, deciding to buy a book of stamps from the newsagent further down the high street.

As she came out of the post office, she saw the elderly gentleman get into a taxi on the corner. The tyres squealed as it sped away. Something lying on the pavement caught Isabel's eye. 'He must have dropped something as he got into the car,' she thought. Isabel waved one of her crutches in the air, trying to catch the attention of the departing taxi, but it was too late. She slowly made her way towards the object and tentatively bent down to pick it up. She was surprised that none of the passing pedestrians offered to help, but they were all in too much of a hurry.

'He's dropped his wallet,' Isabel said to herself.

Her immediate concern was how he would pay the taxi driver when he discovered his wallet was missing. She opened it up to see if there was any means of identification inside. There were three rather dog-eared £5 notes, an old train ticket, a till receipt from the local supermarket and a sweet wrapper that had been very neatly flattened out and folded. But there were no credit cards, driving licence or any other means of identification. Isabel shivered. She decided to buy the stamps, post the letter and then go into the local café for a coffee – then she would consider what to do about the wallet.

Half an hour later, Isabel sat huddled over a coffee. She'd almost forgotten about the wallet; it was only as she felt in her pocket for her phone, to text Karen, that her memory was jogged. Once again she opened the wallet and thumbed through its contents. Not having opened the compartment for loose change she decided to investigate this last hope for some means of identification. At first she thought it was empty, until she delved deeper.

'Oh, what's this?'

She spotted something tucked into the bottom corner, reached in with her fingertips and lifted out a very dainty but expensive-looking ring. Aware that people were looking, she hastily replaced the ring securely and put the wallet back into her pocket. Then she loosened her collar, feeling rather warm now.

'It's a long walk up to the police station – especially on crutches – if this ring is only a worthless piece of costume jewellery,' she thought to herself. 'If I take it into the jewellers on the way, I can see if it's worth taking into the police; if it's not, then perhaps I'll just hand it in at the post office.'

Isabel gulped down her coffee, paid the bill and made her way to the local jeweller. Tentatively she approached the counter. A grey-haired gentleman peered over the top of his reading glasses.

'What can I do for you, madam?'

Isabel explained the situation and retrieved the ring from the wallet. 'I wonder if you could give me some idea of the value of this ring, then, please?'

He picked it up carefully with one hand and held his magnifying glass with the other. Eventually he looked up.

'You have a very fine ring here, young lady. It's very old, very pure gold and some excellently cut diamonds.'

Isabel could feel the sweat running down her back. 'How valuable is it?'

The gentleman fumbled through a small, glossy publication for a few minutes. 'It's probably worth up to £10,000.'

Isabel smiled and thanked him for his help, deciding what to do next. It briefly went through her mind that she was clutching a ring that, if sold, would help to pay the deposit for a mortgage on the equestrian centre.

She tapped some numbers into her phone.

When Isabel arrived home just before lunch, Karen greeted her as she got out of the taxi. They went into the house together.

'I still think you're crazy,' Karen told her. 'There was no means of identification. Who could have blamed you for bringing the wallet home and selling the ring?'

'It wasn't ours, so I took it into the police station. I expect that will be one of the first places that the old gentleman will go to when he realises he's lost the wallet.'

At that moment the house phone rang. Isabel reached across to the kitchen dresser and picked up the handset.

'Hello?' Isabel listened for a moment before replying, 'That's fine. Thank you.' She turned to Karen, grinning from ear to ear. 'Guess what?'

'What?'

'That was the police. The old gentleman has been in to claim the wallet and he wants to bring round a £20 reward – personally – sometime next week. Isn't that good?'

Karen repeated the words, '£20! Only £20! Would you believe it?'

Ben walked in. 'Have I missed something?'

Over a lunch of tomato soup, rolls, cheese and assorted cold meat left over from the weekend, Karen asked, 'Did you get the letter posted OK, after all that?'

Isabel nodded.

'We might still be dependent on Aunty Florence's generosity now that you've given away £10,000 worth of antique ring. Oh, I forgot, we've got a £20 reward coming next week.'

Ben intervened. 'I think you're being unreasonable. £10,000 is a lot of money but it isn't enough to get us out of trouble. Anyway, Isabel did the right thing – don't knock her for it.'

Karen looked annoyed.

'For goodness, sake,' Ben went on, 'there's little enough honesty in the world today as it is. How would you have felt if you'd lost your engagement ring? Wouldn't you have wanted someone to be honest enough to take it into the police station?'

'All £225 worth? I don't think I'd…' Karen stopped. 'I'm sorry.' She sighed. 'I suppose we just wait now, and see if Aunty Florence will be prepared to slum it sufficiently to come and stay.'

With a mouth full of bread roll and corned beef, Ben said, 'Did we get a Christmas card from her last year?'

Karen got up from the table and began to root in the end drawer of the kitchen dresser. 'I really do need to have a good clear out… Ah, here it is.'

It was a very expensive-looking card, with red embossed lettering and a photograph of an apparently well-to-do retired lady.

Isabel looked closer at the slim, rather prim and proper-looking woman in the photo. 'She's wearing some very old-fashioned clothes. Is this an old photograph?'

Karen laughed. 'Even though she's only in her mid-sixties, she dresses like someone from the 1950s. She loves going round car boot sales and charity shops, buying up vintage clothes and memorabilia.'

'Did you send her a card?' Isabel queried.

Karen hesitated. 'I don't think we did.'

'Well, that's a good start!'

Changing the subject, Karen thought out loud, 'We haven't heard any more from Crawford-Smith. Do you suppose no news is good news?'

Ben got up, ready to get back to his desk in the study. 'Quite the opposite. I think he's probably hard at work, scheming, at this very moment.'

Six

The following Monday Isabel was hobbling around the yard on her crutches. She was making her way over to Diana's stable, to make a fuss of her before Alec put her out in the meadow.

'We need to decide what to do with this mare,' Isabel commented to the young groom as she leaned over the door, rubbing the horse's nose affectionately. 'I shan't be riding again for a while.'

Alec tentatively replied. 'I hope you're not thinking of selling her.'

'Of course not! I just thought I might loan her out or something.'

Diana neighed loudly as Alec prepared her to go out. Then, just as he was about to unbolt the stable door, he glanced across the yard.

'Look at that!' he pointed. 'That's a year or two old!'

Isabel looked across to the drive and was surprised to see a small black classic car drawing into the yard. The door opened and an elderly gentleman got out.

'It's the man whose wallet I found. I expect he's got my £20 reward.'

Sure enough, he was clasping something that looked like a 'Thank you' card in his left hand, but whatever was he carrying in the other? Isabel waved until she had caught his attention, and then slowly made her way over to where the small, grey-haired man was standing. By this time, whatever he had been holding in his right hand had been forced into his coat pocket.

'My dear, you must be Isabel!' he exclaimed. 'My name is Archie Johnson.'

'Pleased to meet you.'

To her surprise, Archie took her hand and flamboyantly kissed it. 'The pleasure is all mine.'

Isabel felt herself blush a little, and indicated for him to come into the house. 'You will stay for coffee, won't you?'

Karen was in the kitchen. 'Meet Archie. He was the person who lost the wallet I found the other day.'

Karen smiled, but under her breath whispered, 'Last of the big spenders.'

As Archie sat down at the kitchen table, he held the card out towards Isabel. 'I can't thank you enough for your honesty, young lady. A lot of people would have probably kept the wallet and everything in it.'

Karen placed a tray of coffees on the table. 'Help yourselves to milk and sugar.'

Isabel opened the card. A £20 note dropped out, as had been promised. 'Thank you. You didn't have to.'

After putting a third teaspoonful of sugar into his coffee, Archie said, 'I've brought you something else as well.'

He wrestled with his coat pocket, eventually pulling out a very strangely wrapped package. 'It's nothing to get too excited about,' he smiled, as he handed it to Isabel. 'Do open it.'

She struggled to pull the sticky tape off, worried that she might damage whatever was inside. 'How unusual!' she exclaimed, as she held up a small trinket box.

Archie took a wedding photograph from his pocket. The man in the picture was small, probably in his twenties and very good-looking. The woman was petite and attractive, with her hair piled up and backcombed; it was obviously taken in the early 1960s.

'It's me and my Maggie, on our wedding day,' Archie announced proudly. 'Married in 1962… and she was killed in a car accident in 1971. It's her ring that I carry about in my wallet – means everything to me! I don't know what I'd have done if I'd lost it.'

Isabel listened intently to the story.

Archie dabbed at a teary eye with his large white handkerchief. 'Inside the trinket box is one of my business cards – so you don't lose it. I'm retired now, but if ever my expertise could be of use to you, please call on me.'

Isabel took the card out. 'A solicitor!' But why the trinket box? It seemed a strange gesture. She offered it back.

'No, no… It was precious to my Maggie. I would like you to have it as a gift. I'm sure you have all sorts of jewellery you could keep in it. I felt a bit mean just giving you a £20 note.'

'Thank you.' Isabel placed the little box carefully onto the table, respecting its sentimental value.

Archie broke the silence. 'What happened to your leg, young lady?'

'A muntjac ran out in front of the car. I braked, the car skidded…'

'Oh dear!' Archie replied, pausing briefly before gulping down his last mouthful of coffee. 'Now, you will call me if you need any legal advice? There will be no charge, of course.'

After chatting for a while longer, Isabel waved Archie off and returned to the kitchen to clear up. It was while Isabel was wiping down the worktop that the phone rang.

Before she even had a chance to say anything, a voice bellowed at her, 'It's your aunty Florence here. Don't know what possessed you to suddenly get in contact again. I'm coming tomorrow. Pick me up at the station in Norwich at two o'clock – if you can still recognise me after all this time. And don't be late!'

Isabel cringed. 'What have we done?'

Isabel and Karen stood on the station platform. The wind whistled around them. True, it was warmer than it had been of late, but there was a cold breeze coming off the sea. Karen shivered.

Isabel glanced at her phone. 'Two o'clock!'

'Here it comes.' Karen pointed in the distance.

Sure enough, a train was wending its way along the track towards the platform.

'Has she ever been married?' Isabel asked.

'Married!' Karen shook her head. 'You're kidding! No one would ever want to marry Aunty Florence.'

'That's a bit mean.'

'Mean? You just wait until you meet her.' Karen added grumpily, 'You know I'm not as kind-hearted as you, Isabel.'

'She's probably just lonely. Besides, we need her help; just remember that.'

Moments later, people began to scurry along the platform towards the barriers, dragging huge cases behind them. Isabel looked at Karen. 'Can you see her coming?'

She shook her head. 'I think everyone is off the train now. I don't understand it.'

Then the guard dismounted from the train carrying a large brown dented and scuffed leather suitcase.

'What's wrong, Karen?' Isabel asked. 'You look terrible.'

'She's done it again.'

'What?'

'That has to be her suitcase – nobody else would have a pre-war suitcase – one she's picked up cheap from a charity shop or car boot sale somewhere. She's obviously instructed the guard to carry her case for her, like a servant!'

Sure enough, seconds later a gaunt, severe-looking lady in a below-the-knee black dress, with her hair tied back in a tight bun, dismounted from the train.

'Look, now she's pointing her finger, telling him where to go… how embarrassing.'

Isabel giggled. 'She's giving him quite a rough time, isn't she?'

Karen turned round, as if to walk away.

'You can't leave her behind, she's your aunt.'

At that moment, a gruff voice bellowed, 'Put it down there, young man.'

Obediently, the guard carefully placed the case in front of Karen, and made a hasty retreat.

'Hardly recognised you, Karen,' Aunty Florence commented. 'You look peaky.' Then she pointed accusingly at Isabel. 'Is this a friend of yours?'

Isabel smiled and introduced herself. 'I'm very pleased to meet you. May I call you Aunty Florence?'

Their visitor frowned. 'If you must!'

All the way home, Aunty Florence grumbled.

'It's terribly flat here! I do hate these narrow twisty roads! I hope this house of yours is warm. I can't do with skimping on the central heating. I'm not a lover of Norfolk; it's so off the beaten track!'

Isabel sensed that Karen was biting her tongue, trying desperately not to respond to her aunt in a way that would make her antagonistic towards helping them out.

As for Isabel, she was convinced that Aunty Florence must have some good qualities, and she was determined to find them, over the next few weeks. She would take it on as a new challenge – she would treat her with love and respect and watch what happened.

At last Karen steered the car into the drive. 'Here we are!'

Ben came out, politely opened the door for Aunty Florence and attempted a very low bow – good enough for royalty. Then he kissed the old lady on the cheek.

'Welcome to our humble abode.'

Aunty Florence glared at him but said nothing.

The rest of the day was relatively uneventful as the guest began to settle in, until Isabel was downstairs on her own, late in the evening.

Everyone had gone to bed, and she decided to make that all-important phone call.

She took a deep breath. 'Hello, Mum.'

'Isabel? It's really late, you know. Your father and I were in bed. Couldn't you have called at a more reasonable hour?'

'Please, Mum. I need to talk.'

There was a long silence. 'You want to talk now, do you?'

Isabel heard her father passing comment in the background, obviously aware that it was her. It had been a while and, yes, it was Isabel who had finally broken the contact – although things had not been good for a long time.

'I've missed you over the last few months, Mum; can't we put the past behind us and start again?'

Isabel's father came on to the phone. 'Why now? Has something happened?'

'Dad… How are you?'

He grunted. 'You haven't answered my question yet. Has something happened?'

Isabel hesitated. 'Well, I've had an accident – but I'm still alive to tell the tale.'

Suddenly the line went dead. Tears of regret and disappointment trickled down Isabel's cheeks. 'He hung up! My own father hung up on me!'

That night Isabel cried herself to sleep.

Seven

It turned out that Aunty Florence was an early riser. At 5am her alarm clock echoed throughout the whole house.

Isabel woke up with a start. 'Whatever…?'

Moments later she heard heavy footsteps across the landing, followed by the bathroom door slamming shut. Then, a couple of minutes afterwards, the toilet flushed and the elderly plumbing began to whine and vibrate as Aunty Florence turned the washbasin taps on full. Isabel attempted to turn over and try to get back to sleep for another hour, but the bathroom door creaked open, and she heard voices. It was Karen; Isabel reasoned that she had obviously got up to investigate the commotion. Isabel listened.

'There's no need for you to get up this early. I thought you would probably lie in for a bit this morning.'

'Can't do with lying in bed all day long. I haven't come here to do nothing,' Aunty Florence retorted. 'I intend to make a few changes. You've always been disorganised. You need someone to take charge of things!'

Isabel was surprised that Karen didn't give her aunt the sharp end of her tongue. Knowing Karen, she was probably saving it for later.

Isabel and Aunty Florence had already been hard at work preparing breakfast by the time Karen and Ben arrived downstairs. Isabel was dressed, but Aunty Florence was in a burgundy candlewick dressing gown and blue furry slippers – her grey hair dangling in a long, scraggly ponytail.

'Good job I've brought some proper breakfast ingredients with me,' Aunty Florence said dogmatically. 'Nothing like porridge served with a tablespoonful of bran and a handful of dried figs and prunes.'

Ben had obviously been hoping for a fried breakfast before heading off to the Norwich office.

'No sausages, then?'

Aunty Florence looked sternly at him, and then poked his non-existent paunch. 'It's about time you thought about your health and weight, young man.'

'I didn't know you cared.'

Aunty Florence grimaced. 'And what makes you think I do, after what you did to me five years ago?'

Everything went quiet. Isabel sensed that there was some kind of skeleton in the cupboard.

'Am I missing something?'

Karen quickly changed the subject. 'Well, I'm going to try some of this porridge that Aunty Florence has made. It looks…'

'Me too,' Isabel said, enthusiastically, following Karen's lead, but at the same time wondering what had happened five years previously.

After breakfast, Aunty Florence occupied the bathroom for what seemed like the rest of the morning. By the time she came down the stairs, dressed in a very formal dark skirt – looking like a prim governess from the 1950s, Isabel thought – Ben had left for the office, Karen was in the yard, and only Isabel remained in the house.

'I've ordered a taxi,' Aunty Florence announced. 'You can take me out to lunch and show me your local shopping centre.'

Isabel was surprised. Especially when Aunty Florence added, 'And that nephew-in-law of mine can pay. I'll give him the bill later. He needn't think he's going to sponge off me.'

Karen walked in. 'Oh, you're dressed!'

Isabel glanced at her friend, conscious that the remark sounded a little confrontational. 'Aunty Florence and I are going to have lunch in town. Won't that be nice?'

'I don't suppose you're free?' Aunty Florence questioned Karen. 'That husband of yours is treating us, but he doesn't know it yet.'

Karen looked irritated by the remark but simply replied, 'Sorry, I'm busy today. I have a lesson to take this morning, and I need to ride Henry this afternoon.'

Later on, Isabel and Aunty Florence sat in a little restaurant eating lunch. It had an olde worlde charm about it. There was a high shelf all around the little room, filled with a huge assortment of novelty teapots. All the tables were decorated with pretty red and white tablecloths and the saucers adorned with doyleys.

Aunty Florence leaned forward, her pearls nearly dangling into her tuna salad. 'Tell me, how did you meet that niece of mine?'

Isabel finished her mouthful of lettuce. 'It was about two years ago. I was still at school. We met at a show jumping course down in Newmarket. The horse Karen was riding ducked out of a jump at the last minute, and she kept going, straight into the middle of it. Poles tumbled all around her. She was very fortunate that she wasn't too badly hurt. Anyway, I volunteered to accompany her in the ambulance to the hospital for a check over, just to be on the safe side.'

'Had she broken anything?'

Isabel smiled. 'Only bruising, but she was very sore for a week or two.' She paused thoughtfully. 'I suppose we just clicked, even though we were quite different personalities, but we both love horses and were desperate to make that into a career. Even though Karen is eight years older than me, we became great friends, kept in contact and planned to run an equestrian centre together. After she had taken over the lease for what is now Henry's Stud and Equestrian Centre, she promised me a job as soon as I left sixth form college.'

'Just like that?'

Isabel was puzzled. 'Sorry?'

The older lady scowled as she clarified her point. 'She set up an equestrian centre, without another thought…'

'Not at all, she thought a great deal,' Isabel laughed. 'For a few weeks, anyway. Some things you just know are right.'

Aunty Florence raised her voice, causing the rest of the diners to look round. 'Let me finish!' She drew breath. 'As I was trying to say, these matters take a lot of planning – not something to be done on a whim.'

'But…'

'So how is it all going?' Aunty Florence asked. 'This whim of yours and Karen's?'

Isabel felt as if Aunty Florence's eyes were probing right into her mind. She wasn't sure how much to reveal about the situation at the centre. The plan had been not to say anything about their problems for a few days to allow Aunty Florence to settle in first.

Isabel coughed to clear her throat. 'Well, things are going quite well… in general.'

'Things are going quite well… in general. What does that mean? That sounds a bit iffy to me.'

'Well… um… we've got a fantastic stallion – Henry. And I have a mare that seems to have great potential. And… and… we have a number of livery customers, and a riding school that seems to be very popular.'

'But?'

'But,' Isabel paused, 'there are one or two problems which I am sure Karen will share with you sometime soon.'

At that point the waitress arrived to take their plates.

'Would you like to see the dessert menu?'

'Of course we would,' Aunty Florence replied, in a very loud voice.

Obviously flustered, the waitress returned with one for each of them.

'The dessert of the day is bread and butter pudding,' she said, nervously, 'with cream or custard.'

After placing their orders, Aunty Florence suddenly broached the topic that Isabel had been dying to ask her about. 'If you've known Karen for two years, I expect you know all about Ben's little escapade five years ago?'

'To do with what?'

'Obviously not,' the older lady concluded, before remarking quite bluntly, 'Well, maybe Karen will decide to share that with you sometime soon.'

Isabel smiled politely. 'Touché, Aunty Florence!'

After lunch, Isabel led the way to the newsagent, in order that Aunty Florence might purchase a large notebook and a set of highlighters.

'When we arrive back at the house, I intend to begin writing a long list of changes that need to be made around the house and stable yard, and some procedures that need to be followed to maximise efficiency,' Aunty Florence told her.

Isabel felt anxious about the implications. 'Is that wise?'

'And why not? I intend to help my niece, even though she hasn't asked me to.'

'But you've only just arrived. You don't know anything about the running of the house or yard.'

Aunty Florence smiled in a knowing sort of way. 'That's where you come in. Over the next day or two, you will show me around and explain things.'

'But…'

'I'm not stupid. I know that something is wrong. Karen and I have never been close, especially since she's been married to that waste of space, Ben. She would only have invited me to stay if she was desperate. And my guess is that she wants money… but I know that you're too loyal to her to give anything of that nature away at the moment. Am I right?'

Isabel didn't know how to reply to the comment, so just said, 'Here's our taxi. We'd better hurry.'

The rest of the day passed quietly. Isabel knew that Aunty Florence had seen right through them, that Karen and Ben were anxious not to upset the apple cart, and that Aunty Florence was biding her time. Dinner was polite, and the rest of the evening was spent reading books by the log fire in the lounge.

'I'm going to bed now,' Aunty Florence said in a quiet voice as she carefully folded the corner of the page over to keep her place. 'Goodnight.'

'Goodnight,' they said, in unison.

Aunty Florence hadn't forgotten to charge the day's activities to Ben; every detail had been written down in her large notebook, together with a number of observations and thoughts. She said she would give him a bill in due course.

As she passed Isabel, Aunty Florence bent over and whispered into her ear, 'It's nice to be wanted, even if it is only for money!'

Isabel forced a smile.

Karen looked over the top of her book, once her aunt had left the room. 'Have you contacted your parents yet, Isabel?'

But Isabel didn't answer. She didn't want to admit just how bad things had become between them.

When she went to bed, she called out to God.

> *Hi God. I can't pull the wool over Your eyes. You know exactly what's going on with the relationship between my parents and me. Don't tell me: I have some more forgiving to do. I know that, but please help Dad and Mum to accept me as I am. I know You can mend relationships.*

She paused before saying a long and heartfelt, *'A-m-e-n.'*

Eight

Isabel was getting fed up with her enforced inactivity. As she stood at the stable door of her beloved Diana, rubbing the horse's neck fondly, she was dying to be able to ride her again.

'I'll give you a leg up,' Alec volunteered, brushing back his unkempt blond hair.

'Would you?' Isabel replied, excitedly.

Alec grinned.

Isabel was hurt. 'You were joking, weren't you?'

Alec seemed to move to put his arm round her, but apparently thought better of it. 'Your leg is in full-length plaster – of course I was joking. Besides, you're wearing a skirt.'

'I feel so useless.' It was not really by choice that Isabel was wearing a skirt – she much preferred to be in jodhpurs or trousers – but a skirt was easier to wear with her plaster cast.

There was a commotion outside the back door. 'I think you're needed over there,' Alec observed. 'Karen's aunt is quite a character, isn't she?'

Isabel sighed, picked up her crutches from a nearby bale of hay and began to make her way across the yard. 'You could say that.' She spotted the large notebook in Aunty Florence's hand. 'Here comes trouble.'

'Isabel,' Aunty Florence summoned her. 'I need you to show me around the whole establishment and explain it all to me. I will make notes as we walk round.'

Isabel looked across to Karen. 'Is that OK?'

'I suppose so.' Her friend sighed loudly.

And so began an exhausting morning. Aunty Florence wanted to know every single detail about everything. A very tired and stressed Isabel sat down to a bowl of tomato and basil soup at lunchtime.

'What sort of morning did you have, Aunty?' Karen enquired courteously.

'Very informative. I have listed all my observations and in due course will summarise them and make my recommendations for the necessary changes to take place.'

Karen had clearly had enough. She blurted out, 'What's this all about? Who asked you to interfere?'

Isabel felt for her friend and for Aunty Florence. 'Anyone for a coffee?'

Karen turned to Isabel. 'Not now! There are things we need to sort out.'

'It's a good job I'm not easily offended,' Aunty Florence replied. 'I'm not stupid. I know there's something wrong, and you're probably after money to put it right.'

'Nonsense!' Karen protested.

Isabel glared at her for her dishonesty, believing that an apology would not be out of place. But at that moment, they were interrupted by the doorbell.

'I'll go,' Isabel volunteered, grabbing the opportunity to leave the tension-filled room.

As she pulled open the heavy front door, she was surprised to see two very large men in black suits. One had jet-black hair, the other obviously shaved his head. Isabel felt quite intimidated by them, but she forced a smile.

'Oh – hello. Can I help you?'

The bald one moved forward, into Isabel's personal space. 'We've come on behalf of Mr Desmond Crawford-Smith.'

'Is that right?'

'Yes. Mr Crawford-Smith is a very caring person – he even gives money to charity. As soon as he knew we were coming this way he said, "Make sure that you call in on my friends at

Henry's Stud and Equestrian Centre. Say 'Hi' to them, and tell them that I am not a patient man.'"

Isabel was taken aback. 'Is that a threat?'

The man with black hair smiled menacingly. Isabel nervously stepped back. There was a crash as she knocked a large ornamental jug over with one of her crutches.

Karen appeared. 'Who is it?' She spotted the remains of the broken jug scattered across the floor. 'What's going on?'

The two men smiled. 'It's all right, ladies, we're just going. Don't forget what we told you.'

As the two visitors left, Isabel stood frozen to the spot. Memories of being bullied at school flooded back. She felt that same fear she had experienced as a young teenager in the school playground, fleeing from her pursuers – their threats, the physical pain of every punch, and the words of abuse.

Karen seemed to sense her friend's distress. 'What was that all about?'

As they picked up the broken pieces of china, Isabel relayed what had been said. She felt tears welling up. 'It's not those men… Well, not just those men… It brought back all the feelings I had when I was bullied at school. You know – I told you a bit about it ages ago.'

'Oh. I didn't realise it had affected you so much! Anyway, you're not at school now – that's all in the past.'

Isabel decided to say nothing more on the subject.

As soon as they returned to the kitchen, Aunty Florence demanded, 'What was all that commotion about?'

'Nothing!' Karen replied.

Aunty Florence pointed to the broken china as Karen tipped it into the waste bin. 'If it was nothing, how did that end up in pieces, and why does Isabel look so pale?'

'We're going to have to tell her,' Isabel insisted, 'and Ben when he comes home.'

And so, Karen and Isabel sat down and told Aunty Florence the whole story. 'I see. I knew something was wrong and I guessed it was money that you were after.'

'Well?' Karen said, rather pointedly.

'Well what?'

'Are you going to invest some of your money in the centre?'

Isabel felt embarrassed at her friend's bluntness. 'Karen!'

Karen forced the word, 'Please?'

Aunty Florence frowned, and rested her elbows on the oak table. She pondered for a moment. 'It seems to me that your more immediate problem is not the money; it's dealing with this fellow who's sending his minders to threaten you.'

Ben got back in the early afternoon to finish his working day at home.

'Karen has something to tell you,' Aunty Florence announced to him, as soon as he came in the back door.

'She hasn't fallen off that horse of hers again, has she?'

'I'm glad you find the idea an opportunity for humour. Now, be quiet and listen to what she has to say, young man. This is very serious.'

Ben sat down on the old armchair at the head of the table. The others gathered round.

Aunty Florence looked at Isabel. 'You tell him what happened at lunchtime.'

After Isabel had spoken about the incident with the two men, Karen added, 'So we need to sit down this evening and decide what to do about the situation.'

Ben looked uneasy. 'You need to report this to the police, immediately.'

'He's right for once!' Aunty Florence responded.

'I've got to slip into town. I'll go into the police station while I'm there,' Isabel promised.

Karen volunteered to drive her.

A few minutes later, with Isabel stretched out on the back seat of the small loan car, Karen drove slowly up the road.

'I'd never realised that all the bullying stuff was so significant in your life,' Karen remarked.

Isabel began to wish that she hadn't said anything earlier. 'It's not important.'

'I'm just concerned,' Karen told her. 'That's all.'

Isabel was silent. Things began to flash through her mind, almost as if she were back in the playground. She pictured the group of girls coming towards her. Should she run or hold her ground? It was never just one against one; always three. Her pursuers had that look on their faces: boredom, contempt, power over another – ready to feed off her terror. Once again she considered running. The library was usually safe, or the corridor outside the music room – no one went there during break… But it was too late; her pursuers were almost on to her. She could feel the sweat running down her back. They were getting closer – it was definitely too late to run now… She could hear the words of contempt and see the poised fists – people like that could smell terror from a mile away.

'No, please!' Isabel cried out.

'What?' Karen replied. 'What don't you want me to do?'

Isabel looked up, and felt embarrassed – the fear and hurt were still there; it was still so real. 'Nothing.'

Karen hastily changed the subject. 'So what do you think about my aunt now?'

Isabel took a deep breath. 'She's a forceful woman and I don't know if she is going to be separated from her money easily.'

'I don't know if I want her to be separated from her money easily,' Karen reasoned. 'Imagine spending the next however many years being dictated to by her – with her lists of improvements. I'd rather go bank…'

Isabel stopped her. 'You know you don't mean that. Anything is better than the centre closing down.'

Karen bit her lip. 'I've yet to be convinced of that.'

'What are the options?'

'I don't know, but Aunty Florence was right, the more immediate problem is Crawford-Smith.'

'Your aunt was asking me all about how we'd first met.'

Karen looked thoughtful. 'I suppose we were both quite vulnerable. It was just after my parents had died, and…'

'And I had decided that I wanted a career with horses, much to the disgust of my parents. They both wanted me to get a degree in law, and become a solicitor.'

'Didn't you ever want to go to university?'

Isabel gazed out of the window. There was a moment of silence before she spoke, changing the subject. 'What has your aunt got against Ben? What's he supposed to have done?'

Karen was quick to answer. 'Nothing much; it was just a bit of a misunderstanding.'

There was a pause, while Isabel waited for further explanation. 'And?'

'And… nothing really.'

Everything had been uneventful at the centre when the two girls arrived home later on.

'What have you made for dinner, Ben?' Karen asked.

'It's no good relying on him,' Aunty Florence commented. 'I've prepared a nice hot stew. The potatoes are cooking as we speak.'

Isabel nudged her friend.

'That sounds wonderful,' Karen responded obediently.

'What did the police say?' Ben asked.

Isabel began to unzip her coat as she balanced precariously against the wall. 'They were very helpful; took all the details and said that they would check it out. And they told us to let them know if anything else happens.'

Then Ben picked up a slip of paper near the phone. 'Oh, yes. Someone called Stan phoned. He said he was an acquaintance of Isabel's. He reckoned he was coming to visit tomorrow afternoon. There's a number there, just in case it's not convenient.'

Isabel was a little surprised. 'Oh! I gave him the centre's number when I was in hospital – he seemed very interested in the horses. I didn't really think he'd come.'

Later that evening, Isabel was alone in her room. She could feel herself nodding off as she lay stretched out on her bed. Her eyes became increasingly heavy. She struggled to see the clock on the old mantelpiece – nearly 9.30pm. It seemed later than that. Suddenly she sat bolt upright as her phone rang unexpectedly.

'Hello? Mum?'

Isabel strained to hear as her mother whispered into the phone, obviously anxious not to be overheard. 'Now listen carefully. Your father doesn't know I'm ringing you. You wouldn't have phoned the other day if something wasn't very wrong. Now tell me what it is.'

'I told you. I had an accident,' Isabel told her mother. 'I've broken my leg.'

There was a moment's silence. 'I didn't realise it was serious! I'm so sorry.'

'I really miss you and Dad. Can't we put the past behind us?'

'All that money your father spent on sending you to a good school, and then you threw it all away by working with smelly old horses. You know your father was mortified – after working hard all his life to pay for your education!'

'But Mum, you know I hated school. I was bullied mercilessly while I was at the private school, before I went to the sixth form college – you know that. I told you and Dad, but you never did anything about it.'

'Oh, don't bring all that up again. Why would they bully you, unless you'd done something to upset them first?'

'Mum! How could you say that? You know that bullies pick on people just for being different in some way.'

'So what made you so different that the bullies picked on you?'

Isabel fought back the tears. 'Perhaps it was because I was quiet, studious, not particularly confident. I don't know! Maybe it was because I was a Christian.'

'Oh, don't let's get on to that!'

There was a long silence, which was eventually broken by Isabel. 'And I'm not throwing away my life on horses, either.'

Her mother sighed. 'I can't talk to you while you're like this. I'll phone again in a few days' time. Besides, I can hear your father coming.'

The call finished, leaving Isabel feeling very alone.

Nine

It was only eight o'clock in the morning when the doorbell rang. Karen and Alec were out feeding the horses, Ben had left on a business trip to London and Aunty Florence hadn't yet emerged, for a change, so Isabel slowly made her way to the front door.

'Coming!' she called out from the hall.

The bell rang again, followed by a loud bang. Isabel panicked. 'Maybe those two men have come back!' she thought.

'Who is it?' There was no reply. 'Who is it?'

Then she heard a gentle, softly spoken voice. 'Is that you, Isabel? It's me, Stan.'

Isabel hurriedly leaned her crutches up against the wall and unlocked the door, with great relief. She opened it up and, to Stan's surprise, flung her arms around him. 'Stan, it's so good to see you! Do come in.'

As they went through in to the kitchen, Aunty Florence had appeared and was switching on the kettle. To Isabel's surprise, she looked a little embarrassed at being caught in her dressing gown and slippers by a visitor.

'Oh, you must excuse me.' She pulled her hair back, in what appeared to be an effort to make herself look a little more presentable. 'I'll make some tea and porridge, and then go and get dressed.'

'That's quite all right,' Stan reassured her. 'It's my fault for arriving so early – a friend offered to drop me off on his way to work.'

'This is Stan. I met him in hospital,' was Isabel's belated introduction. 'Stan, this is Karen's aunt – Florence.'

'Anyone for porridge?' Aunty Florence asked.

Isabel hesitated. 'Maybe not today, thank you.'

'I'd love some, please,' Stan said enthusiastically. 'I didn't really have time for breakfast before I came out.'

'Would you like it with a little bran, and some dried figs and prunes mixed in?'

Stan beamed from ear to ear. 'Sounds fabulous!'

Isabel sighed as she poured out the tea. 'Two of a kind,' she muttered under her breath.

Over breakfast, Stan began to tell Aunty Florence about his elderly neighbour, Roy. 'He's not at all well at the moment.' He hesitated. 'Well, he's not so much ill as very frail. I do wish his son would come and visit him from time to time, for Roy's sake. I've never even met the son, although I have spoken to him on the phone – once!'

Isabel noticed that Aunty Florence was conjuring up a very different side to her character. 'That's really sad,' she said, compassionately. 'Does the son live abroad or something?'

Stan shook his head. 'No, but he does travel a lot for his work. I'm not sure what he does, but Roy speaks very highly of him. He always says, "My son passes on his thanks to you, for all you do to help me."' He sat silent for a moment. 'It's a nice thought, but I don't suppose he even bothers about what goes on here in Norfolk. But maybe I'm being a sceptic.'

'I'll take you out to see the horses now,' Isabel promised.

Stan laughed. 'We'll appear a good advertisement for the equestrian centre, won't we? You walking about on crutches with your leg in plaster, and me with my arm in a sling.'

'I can't wait to show you Diana – you'll love her! And I'll share an idea with you that I've got for the centre's future, based on what we were talking about in hospital.'

'Sounds exciting!'

After lunch, Isabel felt a little rude leaving her guest in the hands of another person.

'Are you sure you don't mind? Only there are things I need to see to concerning the yard.'

'That's absolutely fine,' Stan assured her.

Aunty Florence seemed particularly amenable to the idea. 'You be just as long as you like, Isabel. I'm sure we'll be OK.'

'Yes.' Stan suddenly linked arms with Aunty Florence. 'We will!'

Isabel hurried out in to the yard – well, as much as she could with crutches. She went into the office, to be there to answer the centre's phone, take payments and generally oversee the administrative side of things. The afternoon seemed to slip by really quickly.

Isabel glanced at her phone. 'No! Is that really the time?'

She made her way across to the farmhouse to catch up with her guest. Eventually, she found Aunty Florence and Stan laughing and joking in the lounge, listening to music.

'I'm so sorry to have left you for so long.'

Stan looked up. 'Don't worry. Florence is such delightful company. We've had a wonderful time together.'

Isabel raised her eyebrows. 'That's great!'

'Yes, Stan and I have so much in common,' Aunty Florence added. 'We like the same music, we've holidayed in the same parts of the world, we read books by the same authors, and we're definitely going to meet up again.'

Isabel was speechless.

At least for a few hours that day, Isabel was able to put aside her worries and concerns that had been weighing so heavily just recently. The time passed quickly in the busyness.

'You will stay to tea, won't you, Stan?'

Stan seemed to be very appreciative. As he smiled, it highlighted the little wrinkles in the corners of his eyes. 'I didn't really expect to stay all day, but it's been most enjoyable.

And you must share your idea for the centre with me before I go.'

'Oh yes! I forgot.'

As they all sat down to have tea at the big oak kitchen table, there was a wonderful aroma of toasted cheese.

'It's nothing very special,' Karen said, apologetically.

'It looks wonderful,' Stan responded. 'There's something very appetising about cheese on toast; don't you think?'

With a mouthful of cheese, Isabel began to share her idea, 'You know I love coloured horses – especially skewbald ones like Diana.' Everyone nodded. 'I think they can be underrated. Some people take one look at them and just because they're skewbald or piebald believe that they couldn't possibly be any good for competition work. Using a quality stallion, like Henry, and quality coloured mares, like Diana, we could breed some fantastic coloured competition horses.'

'Are you suggesting that we set it up as a breeding programme?' Karen questioned.

'Why not?'

'Sounds like a good idea.' Stan nodded his head in agreement. 'I too have a soft spot for coloured horses.'

'I suppose it's a good way of getting noticed in the competition world,' Karen reasoned. 'Although using a skewbald mare won't necessarily produce a skewbald foal.'

'I know,' Isabel replied, 'but that wouldn't matter.'

Aunty Florence interrupted the conversation. 'Aren't you forgetting something?'

'What?'

'Unless you get Mr Crawford-Smith sorted out and get some financial backing, this place isn't going to be here much longer.'

A long silence followed as the reality of Aunty Florence's words sank in, which was only broken by Stan's concern for his neighbour. 'It's been a wonderful day, but I really ought to phone for a taxi and get home. Roy will be wondering why I haven't popped round to see him this afternoon.'

'I hope that son of his appreciates all that you do for his father,' Aunty Florence said with conviction.

Stan stood up, and put his napkin down. 'I've got no particular desire to be appreciated or thanked. I just want to do the right thing by my neighbour.'

Isabel could empathise with his desire to do the right thing. She smiled and nodded.

Later on that evening, as Isabel, Karen, Ben and Aunty Florence sat drinking cups of tea around the kitchen table, Aunty Florence quickly seemed to revert to her old self. She showed no compassion as she began to pick on Ben.

'What a lovely man that Stan is, so thoughtful and generous,' she said. 'He's so unlike you, Ben.'

'You've no right to speak to my husband like that,' Karen retorted.

Aunty Florence got to her feet. 'That's where you're wrong, young lady – as you well know.'

Ben sat back. 'Er… Are you off to bed now, then, Aunty Florence?'

Without a word, she stomped out of the kitchen towards the stairs.

'Well, what an ending to a lovely day!' Isabel exclaimed.

'You need to stand up for yourself,' Karen scolded her husband.

Ben shrugged. 'Perhaps she's got a point.'

'Nonsense!'

Isabel felt bewildered. 'Is this still "just a bit of a misunderstanding"?'

Ben sighed. 'It was about five years ago…'

'Nobody needs to know,' Karen interrupted.

'OK,' Ben responded, but he didn't seem happy.

Isabel didn't like to see Karen treat Ben disrespectfully. And she didn't like secrecy – it could be so damaging.

Karen suddenly reached across the table. 'Any more tea in that pot?'

Isabel smiled, not wanting her friend to realise how much she had hurt her with her secrecy. 'I'll boil the kettle again.' She hopped across the kitchen, avoiding the hassle of crutches, to fill up the kettle and put it onto the range to boil. 'By the way, I've got an appointment at the hospital the day after tomorrow, although I don't suppose they'll take this wretched plaster off yet.'

Karen, obviously feeling a little guilty about the outburst, volunteered, 'I'll take you in the car.'

As she went to bed that night, Isabel was feeling saddened at the ending of what had been a good day, and she was anxious not to allow the secret of what had happened between Ben and Aunty Florence to come between her and Karen.

Ten

Next morning, as people came downstairs for breakfast, there was an unpleasant atmosphere. Karen appeared to be upset with Aunty Florence for having had a go at Ben the night before. Ben seemed to be annoyed with Karen for the way she had spoken to him. Isabel was disappointed with Karen for not being open with her – supposedly her best friend. And Aunty Florence appeared to still be bitter with Ben for doing whatever he was supposed to have done, and with Karen for not accepting that Ben was in the wrong because of it.

As Aunty Florence ate her porridge, she announced, 'I've left you to sort out your own breakfasts this morning – that way I can't do anything else wrong!'

'About last night…' Karen began.

Ben sat reading the paper. 'Not now, Karen.'

Suddenly the phone rang. Isabel hopped across the kitchen to answer it, glad of the opportunity to change the focus of the morning.

'Hello, Stan. You got back safely, then. How was Roy?'

'I just wanted to thank you for such a wonderful day yesterday.'

'You're welcome. You must come again.'

There was a long silence. 'Could I have a quick word with Karen's aunt, please?'

Isabel passed the phone over to Aunty Florence. 'Stan wants to speak to you.'

Aunty Florence took the phone into the hall, and the others grinned. They heard her say, 'I had a lovely afternoon, thanks.'

Moments later she returned, looking very pleased with herself. 'Charming gentleman!'

Nothing more was said, although the tension had been broken for the moment.

After breakfast, Isabel phoned for a taxi to take her into town. She had decided to take things into her own hands. The thought of having Aunty Florence invest money in the centre and consequently calling the shots was too much to bear. She would see if she could find either another backer or alternative premises. After all, it was one of the few things she could do to help, while still on crutches.

'Just going into town,' she called over to Karen, who was about to go out and exercise Henry.

'What brought that on?'

Isabel replied, 'Nothing. Speak to you later!'

'You might like to call in at the police station and see if there's any news.'

Aunty Florence was in the bathroom when the taxi arrived, so at least she didn't end up tagging along and making things even more difficult!

The high street was littered with estate agents, so Isabel decided to start at one end and work her way up towards the police station and the coffee shop.

'Hello, madam. How can I help you?' a very smartly dressed middle-aged woman asked, as she looked up from a large computer screen.

'I'm looking for a house with about twenty acres of land, to rent – suitable to use for an equestrian centre.'

The woman turned back to her computer screen. 'Please take a seat while I take a look.'

Isabel sat down in front of the large mahogany desk. 'Obviously, if there are stables and barns already built, that's all the better.'

The woman started to scroll through the files.

'We don't really deal with commercial property,' she apologised. 'But I'll have a look, just in case.' Suddenly, she called through into a little adjoining office. 'Mr Hammond, have you got a moment?'

Isabel heard the sound of a heavy chair dragging across a wooden floor, and an older man popped his head round the door. 'You called, Miss Nicholson?'

A two-way conversation developed between the two agents. 'Yes, I did, Mr Hammond.'

He seemed to be in a hurry. 'I've got someone coming for an appointment in a few minutes.'

'Could I just trouble you?'

'It's no trouble at all, Miss Nicholson.'

Isabel intervened. 'I'm looking for suitable premises to use for an equestrian centre.'

Mr Hammond looked a little indignant, as if Isabel had no right to interrupt his consultation with Miss Nicholson. 'To buy or rent?'

'Rent.'

He began to shake his head. 'We don't really do commercial property.' He looked towards his assistant. 'Did you tell her that, Miss Nicholson?'

'I did, Mr Hammond.'

Isabel sighed loudly, and turned towards the door. It looked like it was going to be a long morning.

'Wait!' Mr Hammond seemed to suddenly receive inspiration. 'Mill Farm.'

Moments later, Miss Nicholson printed off a hard copy of the details.

Isabel turned and reached out her hand to take them. 'May I have a look?'

Four bedroomed house, fifteen acres of land, various outbuildings and a large indoor, heated swimming pool. Only five miles from town.

Isabel was shocked at how expensive the rent was, but gave Miss Nicholson her details and promised to be in touch in due course.

The next three estate agents had nothing even vaguely suitable. Then she came to one that specialised in country houses and farms. Isabel had trouble pushing open the strongly sprung swing door while controlling her crutches. To her surprise, no one came to her assistance. When she eventually reached the reception, a man in a very expensive-looking tweed jacket looked at her in rather a condescending way.

'Do you deal with rental properties?' Isabel queried.

'We do,' the man confirmed, 'but we are a very select purveyor of property.'

Isabel felt quite irritated. 'Meaning?'

'I'm not sure if madam would be able to afford our prices – or, in fact, if our properties would be the kind of thing madam is used to.'

Isabel bit her tongue as she hobbled towards the door. Then she spotted details of the ideal property on the wall, but it confirmed what the man had said about price. There was no way that Karen would ever be able to afford somewhere like that. Despondently, she decided to go for a coffee, and then go on to visit the police station.

She was sitting in a corner when someone came over to her table. She didn't take much notice, till he spoke.

'How are things going, my dear?'

'Archie! I'm fine; never better.'

'Are you sure?'

Isabel smiled. 'A few problems with the business, you know.'

'Well, if I can be of help in any way, just let me know. What would you like to drink? I'm paying.'

As Isabel sipped her coffee, she tried to make polite conversation. But she felt anxious about the future and wondered what the news would be at the police station – if any.

When Isabel arrived home just before lunch, she was untypically feeling a little sorry for herself.

She unburdened to her friend, in the yard, out of Aunty Florence's earshot. 'I really don't know what we're going to do. Ever since your aunt has been here, there seems to have been friction and disagreement – and even if she *is* worth millions, what's life going to be like with her bossing us about for the next ten or twenty years?'

'Look, Isabel, I don't want anything to come between us, but… but there are things that I can't talk about.'

Isabel knew that she was referring to what had happened between Ben and Aunty Florence five years before, but decided to leave it for now. Instead, she spoke about the unfruitful morning she had experienced, finishing up by saying, 'And then all the police could tell me was that they are still investigating the incident with those two heavies, but they have no evidence against Crawford-Smith yet.'

That afternoon, Isabel went over to Diana's stable to sit with her beloved horse. It felt safe talking to her. There wouldn't be any repercussions or conflict.

Perching herself on a bale of shavings in the corner, she poured out her heart. 'So much for my lifelong dream coming true. I really don't know what we're going to do. I couldn't stand spending the next ten years with Aunty Florence breathing down my neck, but there don't seem to be any other options open.' She sighed. 'Not that Aunty Florence has come up with any money yet, anyway. And then there's Crawford-Smith…'

'Are you OK in there?' Alec poked his head over the half-door, his fringe hanging down over his eyes. 'You don't seem your usual cheerful self.'

'Sorry.'

'Do you want to talk about it?'

Isabel was touched by Alec's concern. 'Thanks, but unless you're a secret millionaire, you probably wouldn't be able to help.'

'My uncle has got a paddock and an old barn – you know, if you ended up with nowhere to keep Diana.'

'Thanks, Alec. I might be glad to take up your offer.'

Alec leaned on the half-door. 'When do you go to the hospital about your leg?'

'Tomorrow.'

'Hope it all goes well. You'll feel better when you can ride again.'

Just as Isabel was about to reply, her phone rang.

'Ben? Is something wrong?' There was no reply. 'Is that you, Ben?'

'Isabel, I need to talk to you sometime. Aunty Florence has every right to be bitter against me after what happened.'

'What did happen?'

'Not now. Karen is going out to do a shop at the supermarket this evening. Perhaps we can meet in the tack room for a chat.'

Isabel put the phone into her pocket, intrigued by Ben's mysterious call.

Later that day, perched on top of a pile of jute rugs, surrounded by saddles, bridles and grooming kits, Isabel listened intently as Ben began to explain. He looked embarrassed.

'You must understand that Karen's and my relationship with Aunty Florence was never a good one, but it was better than it is now. I suppose she tolerated us for the sake of her brother – Karen's dad. They were chalk and cheese. He was so gentle and kind.'

'But what could you have done to make her so bitter against you?'

'Nothing, really – you see, it all escalated. It all began at a family wedding. It was one of Karen's cousins – Josh.'

'But, I didn't think that Aunty Florence had any…'

'Oh no,' Ben interrupted. 'Aunty Florence never got married or had children. She was one of five – two boys and three girls. There are loads of cousins.'

'Go on.'

'Aunty Florence thought Josh was wonderful and could do no wrong, just because he was training to be a GP! And poor Karen couldn't do anything right.' Ben drew a deep breath. 'I'd been drinking, and, well, you know what happens after people have had a few too many drinks. I thought I'd tell Aunty Florence a few home truths about her "wonderful Josh".'

'And?'

'And it all got a bit out of hand – things were said that probably shouldn't have been, Aunty Florence got on her high horse, and Karen and I made a hasty exit. There was an attempt at reconciliation a few months later but, as you see, Aunty Florence is still very bitter about it all.'

Isabel was puzzled. 'Seems like an overreaction to me! But if that's true, why is she here now?'

'Perhaps it was because Karen asked her and she was always very close to Karen's dad.' He frowned. 'Or maybe she's just come to cause trouble and get her own back. I really don't know.'

'We really should be going into the house.'

Then – footsteps in the yard!

'Is anyone out here?' a voice called out.

It was Aunty Florence.

Isabel silently sent up an arrow prayer to God:

Hi God. Please don't let Aunty Florence have heard Ben and me talking together. I wouldn't want her to think we were talking about her behind her back. Thanks. Amen.

Eleven

Isabel struggled to carry a hay net at the same time as walking with crutches – fortunately it was only quite a small daytime net. She heaved a sigh of relief as she reached her horse's stable.

'Diana!' She thought it strange the young mare had not put her head over the door when she had heard her approach that morning, but Isabel was shocked at what she saw when she looked into the stable. She spoke softly. 'Hello, what's going on here?' A girl, about eleven years old, stood there, gently rubbing Diana's nose.

As she turned to face Isabel, her red hair, tied into two long plaits, swung across her face. 'I didn't mean any harm. She's my new friend.' The young girl brushed some straw off her blazer with her hand. 'Mum will be cross with me if I mess up my school uniform. And I mustn't upset her – not now!'

Isabel decided to treat her uninvited guest with care.

'This is my horse, Diana, and I'm Isabel. What's your name?'

The young girl shuffled nervously. 'My name's Hannah. I go riding at my aunt's house in Yorkshire when I stay there during the summer holidays. I like horses better than I do people!'

Isabel opened the door, walked into the stable and started to put up the hay net.

'Shouldn't you be at school?' she asked.

Hannah rubbed a tear from her cheek with her sleeve. 'I hate school.'

'Why do you hate school?'

Diana nuzzled her new-found friend, in between tugging hay from the net.

'I wish I could leave school and work with horses.'

'I didn't like school, either.'

'I wish I was like you. You work with the horses, don't you? I've seen you. I've seen the horses when Daddy drives me to school.'

Isabel leaned against the stable door. 'Yes. I wanted to work with horses for a long time, so when I left school last summer, when I was eighteen, I started working here, for my friend Karen.'

There was a pained look on Hannah's face. 'Chloe bullies me at break time. She says horrible things and makes fun of me. I'm really scared of her.'

'Why don't we go into the office? We need to phone your dad to let him know you're safe. He must be really worried. OK?'

The girl looked reluctant. 'OK.'

Half an hour later, Hannah's dad arrived in the car, to take her back to school. Hannah told him what had been happening during breaks.

'I'll speak with the head teacher,' he promised, before turning to Karen and Isabel. 'Her mum's not at all well at the moment and Hannah is really struggling. But I didn't know she was being bullied. Thank you for your kindness.'

'Maybe Hannah would like to come and help with grooming the ponies sometimes on a Saturday,' Isabel suggested. 'She could have a ride on one of the ponies, sometimes, as a kind of reward.'

'We might even be able to teach her to jump,' Karen said, nodding, 'if she makes a good job of the grooming!'

'I'm sure she'd love that, thank you,' her dad said.

'Oh wow – can I?' Hannah cried.

Isabel smiled. 'I'm sure Diana would love to see you.'

Later that day, as Karen drove Isabel to the hospital, Isabel couldn't help thinking about her conversation with Ben the evening before. She thought about the wedding and wondered if such animosity really could have resulted from a few drunken comments. And she wondered if Aunty Florence had suspected that they were talking about her in the tack room.

'What sort of mood was Aunty Florence in this morning, before we left?'

Karen braked sharply to avoid a fat pigeon sitting in the middle of the road. 'She seemed OK. Didn't say much, though. Why?'

'She didn't say anything about hearing Ben and me in the tack room last night, when you were out?'

Karen grinned. 'Oh yes, Ben told me about that. We haven't seen anything of her money yet.'

'Karen, fancy saying that!'

'Oh, don't looked so shocked! Let's be real, the only reason we invited her to stay was to try to get some cash out of her to buy the centre.'

'But she thinks the first thing we need to do is to sort things out with Crawford-Smith before we even think about raising the money to buy the property.'

'So what do we do?'

Isabel thought for a moment before suggesting, 'It was Ben who discovered Crawford-Smith in the first place. Maybe he could make a few enquiries in the financial world to find out something about his planned development around the coast – and if it involves the land where the centre is.'

'Why?'

'Out of interest. He certainly seems eager to get it.'

'OK, I'll have a word with Ben tonight. But I warn you, he'll probably make some excuse about ethics, or the inaccessibility of that kind of information.'

As soon as the hospital came into full view, the shortage of parking also became apparent.

'If we can't get a parking space, I'll just wait with the car,' Karen said.

'Suits me; I'll come and find you later.'

As Isabel made her way up the corridor, she hoped that this might be the end of needing crutches. She turned into the door signposted 'Fracture Clinic'.

She sighed, and mumbled to herself, 'It's packed. I'll be ages.'

Then suddenly she heard a familiar voice behind her.

'Fancy seeing you here today.'

Isabel turned round. 'Stan! Good to see you. How are you?'

There was such a warmth in his brown eyes. 'Can't grumble; there's people worse off than me. How's that aunt of Karen's?'

'I know you have a soft spot for coloured horses, but I do believe you're developing a soft spot for her too.'

Stan's face went red. 'It's really hot in here, isn't it?'

'You can't fool me, Stan! You're sweet on her, aren't you?'

'I would like to see her again. Maybe I could come and visit the centre again one day soon?'

Isabel smiled. 'Of course you can.'

Stan's face lit up. 'Maybe not a whole day. Roy has had a fall – I couldn't leave him all day.'

'But what about Roy's son? You can't be expected to do everything.'

'He's in Canada on business at the moment. So I'm all Roy's got.'

Isabel smiled at him. 'Roy is a very fortunate man to have someone as caring as you for his neighbour.'

Stan produced an old-fashioned diary and pen from the inside pocket of his tweed sports jacket. 'Could I make a date to come over, then, please?'

The next Wednesday was decided upon.

'Make sure Florence is going to be there, won't you?'

'Yes, Stan. I will.'

'So what's happening?' Karen asked Isabel, having found a parking space.

Isabel couldn't hide the disappointment in her voice. 'I've been to X-ray and seen the registrar; it's not healing as quickly as it should, so they're going to remove this full plaster and replace it with a knee-length one. At least I'll be able to put some weight on that – and maybe ditch the crutches; at least some of the time.'

'Shall I get some coffee?' Karen offered.

Isabel nodded. 'It could be up to an hour before I go in to the plaster room. Maybe I can have one of those bright-red plaster casts.'

Moments later, Karen returned with two cardboard cups filled with steaming hot coffee.

'Oh, I meant to tell you, I saw Stan earlier. He's coming over Wednesday.'

Karen grinned mischievously. 'You've got yourself an admirer there!'

'Not me!'

'No. You don't mean…'

'Yes, he really has taken a liking to your aunt.'

Karen began to whistle the 'Wedding March'.

'Now, that is being ridiculous!' Isabel laughed.

'Maybe.' Karen raised her eyebrows. 'Anyway, we don't want her spending all her money on a big wedding, do we?'

Early the following week, Aunty Florence received a phone call. After listening for several minutes, she replied with the words, 'I see!' and finished the call.

Isabel looked round from filling the kettle up for a bedtime drink. Aunty Florence was staring into space.

'Aunty Florence! What's wrong? Is it bad news?'

'That was Stan.' Aunty Florence took a deep breath. 'He won't be coming over for the foreseeable future.'

'Oh no! I am sorry. What's happened?' For a second, Isabel thought Aunty Florence looked vulnerable. This was certainly a side of Karen's aunt that Isabel had not seen before. 'Would it help to talk?'

'It's all happening again,' Aunty Florence whispered.

'What is? Aunty Florence, sit down. Are you all right? Look, I'll make some hot chocolate and we can take it into the lounge so we won't be disturbed when the others come in from checking the yard.'

'Thanks.' Aunty Florence's voice was barely audible.

'And I'll bring that packet of biscuits.'

Isabel steered the older woman into the lounge, made the drinks, then came back and curled up in an easy chair as best she could with her leg in a short plaster cast. Aunty Florence had chosen a more upright chair; Isabel was not too sure if it was a comfort issue, or one of upbringing. There were the remains of a log fire burning in the old brick fireplace and there was still quite a lot of heat coming from the glowing embers.

'So that was Stan on the phone...'

'He's not coming tomorrow. Apparently his neighbour, Roy, has taken a turn for the worse, or so he says – sounds like an excuse to me.'

Isabel dunked a biscuit into her hot chocolate. 'Well, he did say that Roy had had a fall when I bumped into him at the hospital.' She opened her mouth to take a bite of the biscuit. 'Oops!' Hot chocolate splashed onto her lap as the soggy biscuit fell back into the mug.

'He's had second thoughts and he's trying to let me down lightly. And do you blame him?'

Isabel was itching to voice her agreement to the second point, but compassion got the better of her. 'I'm sure he would come if he possibly could.'

Aunty Florence shook her head. 'But you don't understand, dear; I know the signs. I've been there before.'

'You have? With Stan?'

'No, no, not Stan. With Michael Duval. He was a financial adviser: tall, slim, muscular, black wavy hair, red sports car, an apartment in Knightsbridge…'

Isabel sat forward on her chair. 'Oh?'

Aunty Florence took a sip of her hot chocolate. 'We met at a mutual friend's party in London thirty-five years ago. We used to meet once or twice a month and go out to dinner and see a show as well. I loved him to bits and longed for the day when we would get married and settle down together. I never told the family about him – it was my secret.'

'So what happened?'

Isabel was shocked as Aunty Florence's face crumpled. 'He wrote me a letter saying that he had found someone else – someone he worked with. It was going to be a quick wedding. I never saw or heard from him again.'

'Oh, I am sorry!'

'I decided that I would remain single for the rest of my life because I found it so difficult to trust anyone after that. But when I met Stan – well, this sounds silly, but I felt a *spark*. I know it was early days…' Aunty Florence blew on her hot chocolate before reprimanding herself: 'You stupid old woman, Florence: you never learn, do you?'

'But Stan is honest and caring. I think he *does* like you, really I do.'

'I wish I was more trusting, and could see the best in people, like you do,' Aunty Florence replied.

Isabel shrugged. 'Trusting anyone is never easy. You've only just met me; you might change your mind about me when you've known me for a bit longer.'

'I've said too much. Forgive me for bending your ear. I'm going to bed now.'

Aunty Florence left her half-finished hot chocolate, and stood up.

'Thank you for your time, dear,' she said, quite formally. 'You are very kind.'

Isabel reached out and squeezed Aunty Florence's hand in an attempt to comfort her, feeling that she was beginning to get some kind of connection with her friend's eccentric, feisty aunt.

Ben, Karen and Alec came in soon afterwards. 'One of the livery ponies got out of the small paddock and didn't want to be caught again! Just as well he didn't run onto the road.'

'I'll make you some hot chocolate.'

Karen picked up the two mugs and half a packet of biscuits. 'What's been going on here?'

Isabel felt she shouldn't break a confidence, so she simply said, 'Oh, Aunty Florence and I just felt like a sit down with some hot chocolate and biscuits. She's quite sweet, really.'

Karen flung her arms up in a demonstration of mock surprise. 'Since when have you two been such close friends? What's going on?'

'Stan's not coming this week. Roy's not too well.'

Twelve

Isabel looked out of the open bathroom window on hearing the distinctive noise of a diesel engine. Dressed in her most severe 1950s-style outfit, Karen's aunt was just stepping into a taxi.

'Where are you going?' Isabel called. 'It's only eight o'clock!'

Aunty Florence poked her head out of the car window. 'I'll be back in time for lunch.'

With that, the taxi sped out of the drive, creating a shower of dust and gravel.

Isabel went across the landing and shouted down the stairs, 'Karen! What's going on? Where's your aunt going?'

Karen wandered through into the hall, appearing unconcerned. 'She just said that she had to go and get something that she could depend on – whatever that means.'

'But didn't she give you any clues as to where she was going? She was quite upset about Stan, you know.'

Karen shook her head. 'None at all.'

The morning seemed to pass by very slowly. Ben was working from home, so it seemed to be a good time to talk to him about Crawford-Smith. Isabel sat down on the edge of the large mahogany desk that stood in the corner of the study. Karen was hovering in the background.

'We need to speak to you, Ben.'

'I'm rather busy at the moment – can't you see? Besides, I hate it when the two of you decide to gang up on me.'

'This won't wait,' Karen said.

'It's like this,' Isabel began. 'You know that you were our first contact with Crawford-Smith – through the office.'

'Yes, but I didn't know what he was really like,' Ben said, defensively.

'You work in finance, and Crawford-Smith is an investor in property development. He's already had contact with the company you work for. Surely you could make a few enquiries and find out what he's up to?'

'Why?' Ben scowled. 'Anyway, that wouldn't really be ethical.'

Karen gave Isabel a knowing look.

'Besides,' Ben went on, 'I'm only a small cog in the large wheel of financial investment. I've got no influence at all, really.'

'I'll get a lemon meringue pie out of the freezer for dinner tonight – your favourite,' Karen promised.

'See, she does love you,' Isabel grinned.

Ben sighed and sat back in his chair. 'OK. Can I get on with my work now? I've a lot to do before I pop out for an appointment later.'

Karen gave him a big hug. 'Thanks, Ben. I knew you wouldn't let us down.'

It was just before midday when Isabel heard the sound of the taxi coming back into the yard. Moments later the kitchen door flew open with a 'Bang!' Suddenly, Isabel felt her legs being swept from underneath her, and she grabbed the edge of the kitchen table for support. She looked down at a pair of large brown eyes, which were looking up at her. Tentatively, she held out her hand.

'And who might you be?'

Aunty Florence strode into the kitchen, with arms full of doggy accessories. 'Colin, come to Mummy.'

Isabel's mouth dropped open. 'Is he yours?'

Aunty Florence bent down to arrange a colourful padded dog bed in the corner of the kitchen. 'He certainly is. What do you think of him? He won't let me down – not like Stan.'

'What type of dog is he?'

'He's a twelve-week old labradoodle.'

Isabel looked worried. 'What about Karen? Have you asked her if she minds having a puppy in the house?'

Aunty Florence proceeded to fill up the small, plastic water bowl. 'If she objects, I'll just go home.'

Isabel glanced out of the window. 'Well, we'll soon find out what she thinks – she's walking across the yard right now.'

Karen took off her boots at the back door and padded into the kitchen in just her thick woolly socks.

'What is it, you guys? What's going on? Has something happened? Where did you go off to so early this morning, Aunty Florence?'

Karen appeared not to have noticed the dog bed and water bowl on the old flagstones, until she nearly lost her footing. A black dog was lying stretched out at her feet, tugging relentlessly at the toe of her left sock. As she looked down at the puppy, his big brown eyes met with hers, and then he began to wag his tail excitedly.

Karen opened her mouth as if to speak, but was interrupted by Aunty Florence. 'I think he likes you, dear.'

Karen leaned down and stroked the dog gently. He let go of the sock and got up, still wagging his tail. Karen gently picked him up and cradled him in her arms. Isabel watched the tenderness of the scene, feeling a lump in her throat. She was going to comment on her friend's uncharacteristic display of gentleness and spontaneity, but it just came out as, 'Oh, Karen!'

She looked up. 'Isn't he gorgeous?'

Isabel put her hands together. 'Can he stay?'

Aunty Florence grinned. 'He's called Stan. He's more reliable than the human version.'

'I thought you said he was called Colin?' Isabel exclaimed.

'I've changed my mind.'

Karen was still cradling the puppy in her arms. 'Yes, I suppose he can stay, as long as you two clear up any accidental messes.'

'Will Ben mind?' Isabel quizzed.

Karen gently put the little dog back onto the floor. 'Ben's always wanted a dog. He's a big kid at heart!'

Later on, when he arrived home, Ben was informed that Stan was now resident in the farmhouse.

'What?' he said in surprise. 'I thought he was keen on Aunty Florence, but...'

At that moment the little dog came bounding through, wagging his tail.

'Stan the dog!' Karen explained. 'He belongs to Aunty Florence.'

Ben squatted down on the floor and began to have a tug-of-war with the puppy and his squeaky toy. His face lit up.

'But tell us what you found out about Crawford-Smith,' Isabel demanded.

'Ah! You'll never guess what I discovered.'

'What?'

With what appeared to be a deliberate air of mystery, he began to unfold the story. 'It would appear that Mr Crawford-Smith's coming into the office to make some enquiries about financial investments, seemingly bumping into me quite by chance, and finding out about our predicament with the centre and offering his help, was all a set-up. He's had his eye on Henry's Stud and Equestrian Centre and the surrounding land for months now. He's already negotiating deals with our neighbours for their land, and he's been badgering the planners for permission to build a huge holiday village here.'

'But has he got planning permission for it?' Isabel questioned, anxiously.

'Not yet, but the planners seem to be looking quite favourably at the job opportunities such a holiday complex would bring to the area – among other things.'

'What's going to happen to us?' Karen asked.

'Crawford-Smith is spreading the word in investment circles that the project will go ahead. He believes that it's only a question of time, that we'll never raise the money to buy the centre, so it will go up to auction. And then he will pay whatever it costs to buy this place.'

'But…'

Ben interrupted Isabel. 'It would appear that the only reason he came here to meet us and look round was to assess the likelihood of us being able to raise the money.'

'Where does that leave us, and the centre?' Karen queried.

'Nature calls!' Aunty Florence got up to go to the bathroom. Ben appeared to wait until he heard the door slam firmly shut.

'It leaves us desperate enough to do some grovelling to Aunty Florence. She's our only hope!'

Around the highly polished circular walnut dining table were five chairs. In front of each chair was some paper, a selection of pens and a bottle of still mineral water. Karen, Ben, Isabel and Aunty Florence were already seated, waiting.

'So what's this all about?' Aunty Florence asked. 'Save that it is to do with keeping the centre going.'

Isabel swept back her mass of dark hair, tucking it behind her ears in an unruly mess.

'Who is the fifth seat for?' she asked.

Karen smiled. 'Just wait and see.' She hesitated. 'I just want to fix things, and this is the only thing I could think of doing. Our additional guest will not be joining us until later.'

Aunty Florence was displaying one of her 'we are not amused' expressions as she sat at the table in what seemed to be yet another rather old-fashioned, drab black dress. She sat very upright, with a meticulously straight back.

'I don't understand what this is all about anyway,' she muttered.

At that moment, Basil, the stable cat, ran into the dining room meowing loudly with Stan in hot pursuit.

'Are all labradoodles hyperactive?' Ben enquired. 'Yours seems to be, Aunty Florence!'

Karen frowned at him. 'Can you be serious, Ben?'

Isabel tried to lighten the atmosphere. 'I think Basil has discovered a new lease of life since that puppy arrived. Don't you, Karen?'

Karen didn't respond. 'As you might have guessed, the reason we are meeting today is to discuss the future of Henry's Stud and Equestrian Centre. We haven't got long before the premises are auctioned off, unless we can raise more than £500,000 to buy them ourselves.'

'We know that already!' Ben said. 'So what's new?'

Isabel tactfully turned to Aunty Florence. 'Time is getting short now. We need to be making decisions. The thing is this…'

'We need someone rich to bail us out,' Ben interrupted.

'We need some of your money,' Karen told her, bluntly. 'After all, what's £500,000 or so, compared with all your fortune?'

The whole room went silent for what seemed like two or three minutes.

'Come and stay for a holiday – indeed! You only wanted me for my money, all along!'

'You didn't give me a straight answer when I asked you before.'

'You're right, I didn't!'

'Look, we haven't got time to mess about. Will you help us?' Karen demanded.

Isabel cringed at her directness. 'Karen!'

Aunty Florence put her hand on Isabel's arm. 'You're such a kind, polite girl. However did you become friends with the likes of my niece?' She paused. 'The answer is *no*.'

Isabel's eyes darted between her friend and her aunt, with the sudden realisation that in some ways they were actually not too dissimilar.

At that moment the doorbell rang. Karen jumped up. 'It's Desmond Crawford-Smith. I was going to tell him that we have raised sufficient money to buy the centre, and then that would have been an end to it.'

'Oh, Karen!' Ben exclaimed, exasperated.

'So now what do I tell him?'

'That's up to you.' Aunty Florence stood rather abruptly. 'I'll go and make some tea.'

'I was trying to help,' Karen argued. 'I wanted to fix things for us. I…'

Aunty Florence answered the door on the way to the kitchen, and Mr Crawford-Smith barged into the dining room, which was instantly filled with the faint aroma of mothballs. 'Make this quick, I don't have all day. What's this all about?'

Isabel looked across to Ben, and then to Karen.

'Well,' Karen began, 'the reason I contacted you, Mr Crawford-Smith, was because I was hopeful that we would have raised the money to buy this place by now, so we could have told you not to waste any more time preparing plans and raising money for redevelopment, but…'

The bumptious man plonked himself down onto one of the empty chairs. It creaked loudly. 'So, what you are saying to me is that there is no way you can raise the money in time. Why doesn't that surprise me? Well, I can wait until the auction on 15th August.'

'I don't suppose you would consider us being your tenants, would you?' Isabel asked, tentatively.

The man burst out laughing. 'You've got to be joking! I've got plans to redevelop this whole site, so you'd better start packing your bags.'

'Would anyone like a cup of tea and a digestive biscuit?' Aunty Florence brought in a loaded tray, which she placed down carefully, so as not to spill any tea on the polished table.

Mr Crawford-Smith stood up. 'What a waste of time. Just remember: get your bags packed ready to move out on the 15th August – otherwise I'll send some of my employees in to help you.'

Karen and Isabel attempted to follow Mr Crawford-Smith out. 'Is there nothing that will change your mind?' Karen asked, desperately.

But it was too late. The sound of the door slamming shut echoed through the old house. The girls went back to the dining room.

'Tea, Karen?' Aunty Florence glanced at her.

'What?'

'Would you like milk in it?'

'Do you realise what you've just done?' Karen shouted at her. 'Despite all your money, you've left us destitute – and humiliated us in front of that obnoxious man!'

'Me? I rather think that was your doing, dear.'

The next morning, Karen and Ben were up early. As Isabel lay in bed, thinking about the night before, she heard them arguing on the landing.

'You're no support to me,' Karen accused. 'Why did you leave me to deal with Crawford-Smith on my own last night? Are you a man or a mouse?'

'That's hardly fair!'

'Is it fair for me to be humiliated in front of everyone?'

'Your aunt was right. It was you who invited Crawford-Smith. Who in their right mind would invite the one person who is their greatest opposition to a planning meeting? It's just… crazy!'

'So now I'm crazy, am I?'

'Keep the noise down. It's really early, someone might hear.'

Karen laughed loudly. 'You think?'

'Shall I go down and make some coffee?'

'No! I don't want coffee. I want you to sort this whole terrible situation out – right now!' There was a pause. 'And now you've made me cry – I never cry!'

'Look – please don't cry.' Ben's voice was softer now. 'I'll try to sort something out, I really will.'

There was a moment of silence before Isabel heard Karen's muffled reply. 'Perhaps I will have that coffee.'

'I love you.'

'Love you too.'

Thirteen

Later that day, it was a very sombre-looking Aunty Florence who sat in the back seat of a black taxi on her way to the railway station. Torrential rain hammered on the metal roof. She was dressed in the same black dress in which she had arrived; once again, her hair was scraped back in a bun. Filled with sadness, she gazed out of the window, watching the north Norfolk scenery flashing by. Every farmhouse she passed reminded her of what she had left behind at the equestrian centre: most of all, the family she had always wanted but never had. Already she was missing Karen and the others dreadfully, but she tried to console herself in the knowledge that she wasn't truly wanted. She had never really fitted in there – come to that, she had never really fitted in anywhere.

'They only wanted me for my money,' she murmured.

Aunty Florence was aware of the taxi driver glancing at her in the rear-view mirror – she thought perhaps he had heard her whispered comment. She froze for a moment, in the pretence that she had said and done nothing – nothing at all!

Her gaze turned towards the window once again. The pouring rain seemed to exaggerate the greenness of the spring grass, and she realised there was something very beautiful about north Norfolk.

She had found a family here – and lost it. How could she have been so careless? As if by instinct, she looked around for Stan the labradoodle, almost calling out his name, before the realisation came that she had left him behind. After all, he would be a lot better off living in the countryside. What had she been thinking, to go off and buy a puppy like that? Just because she felt rejected! She felt broken-hearted not to have him either, but a small flat in the middle of town was no place for a dog. And then there was his namesake – Stan!

'Stan…' Aunty Florence bit her tongue as the taxi driver glanced into the rear-view mirror again.

'Are you speaking to me, Missus?'

'Is your name Stan?'

'Yeah.'

Aunty Florence frowned, not knowing if she should believe him. 'You just concentrate on your driving, young man.'

He grunted something under his breath which sounded neither polite nor respectful. But Aunty Florence's attention had wandered towards his shirt collar. Dark blue was not a suitable colour to wear when suffering from acute dandruff. She longed to be able to brush the white flecks off.

'How much further is it to the station?'

There was no reply; the taxi driver had begun a conversation on his hands-free phone. Aunty Florence caught a few words: obviously a minor family crisis at home… Yes, 'home'. She had almost come to think of Norfolk as home: living with Karen, Ben and Isabel. She had hoped she might form a close relationship with Stan; she'd so enjoyed his company, and she had thought he had enjoyed hers too. They'd had a real connection, after all.

Her mind wandered off into fantasy. He was a horse lover, so they could have all lived in the big farmhouse together.

But that was just a fairy tale! A silly crush! 'Act your age!' she muttered to herself.

She sighed. Her refusal to hand over more than £500,000 meant that she believed she was no longer welcome at the equestrian centre. But there were reasons for her decision.

She took out her phone and was poised to ring the centre; perhaps not her niece – she could be a bit sharp – maybe Isabel. She was aware of possibly having burned her bridges earlier that morning with her scathing speech accusing her niece of being mercenary, followed by a flamboyant exit, and the words, 'You will never see me again!' Perhaps it had all been a little on the spur of the moment and impulsive – like buying that dog.

But reconciliation was worth a try.

Three times she carefully dialled the number and then hung up at the last moment, before eventually making the call.

She listened carefully, waiting to hear the familiar voice of Isabel, but there was no reply. Aunty Florence felt a strong sense of disappointment. She placed her phone back into her bag, feeling that at least she had tried, but it was too late; she would have to live with the consequences of her rash exit.

The taxi drew to an abrupt halt behind a long queue of traffic. Aunty Florence glanced out of the window. There was a signpost to the railway station – not far now. Every single set of traffic lights seemed to be against them.

Suddenly, Aunty Florence became aware of the warmth of the sun on the back of her neck. She looked out. The rain was easing and a rainbow graced the blue sky.

'Looks as if the rain's going to clear!' she called through to the driver.

He smiled courteously as he turned in to the approach to the station. Moments later the taxi came to a standstill; the noise of the excited travellers outside was masked only by the loud clacking of the diesel engine ticking over. The driver came round and opened the door for Aunty Florence, reaching into the cab to take her pre-war suitcase. But she sat tight and began to wrestle with him for the handle.

'No, leave it. I'm not going. I live at the equestrian centre now. Take me home.'

Fourteen

Aunty Florence's homecoming had been greeted with a variety of reactions. The next morning there was still something of an atmosphere – although Isabel was doing her best to calm the situation.

'You're up and about early,' Karen commented, as Isabel hobbled around the kitchen in her plaster cast, preparing a full English breakfast for everyone.

'I'm just trying to make an effort,' she explained. 'I thought that maybe if we all sat round the table over a meal... well, maybe we could be friends again.'

'Be friends again,' Karen repeated cynically. 'After all that's happened?'

'Aunty Florence chose to come back again because you're family.'

Suddenly Karen's gaze turned to a blue envelope lying on the table, in Aunty Florence's place. 'What's that?'

'It's a letter!' Isabel replied, dryly. 'I found it in the hall from yesterday's post. We must have missed it in all the upset.'

Karen frowned as she picked it up and read, 'Miss Florence Grimes, c/o Henry's Stud and Equestrian Centre. It's marked "personal and confidential". I wonder who it's from.'

'I expect we'll find out in a minute, when your aunt opens it,' Isabel replied logically, as she carefully placed the bacon onto the griddle. 'Can you pass me those sausages, please?'

Karen picked up a polystyrene tray with eight wild boar sausages inside. 'Unusual choice!'

'That bacon smells good.' It was Ben, followed closely by Alec, who looked as if he had just crawled out of bed, as usual.

Alec yawned. He picked up the blue envelope and peered at it. 'Is it Aunty Florence's birthday, then?'

'That's it!' Karen exclaimed. 'It must be a birthday card for Aunty Florence.' She took the envelope from Alec and held it up to the light before commenting disappointedly. 'It looks more like a letter, and anyway, it doesn't feel stiff enough to be a card – not unless it's one of those cheap folded paper things.'

'Does it matter what it is? It's not yours,' Ben said, crossly.

Isabel carefully took the envelope and put it down on the table once again, just as Aunty Florence came in. Dressed in her usual black, she used her words sparingly. 'Morning. What's for breakfast... oh, a letter for me. I wonder who it's from.' She examined the envelope carefully, even to the extent of smelling it, before laying it down on the table. 'It's a very good-quality envelope and it smells of pine disinfectant – and what lovely handwriting! Obviously someone with a good education.'

Isabel began to dish out the breakfasts: bacon, egg, sausage, beans and tomatoes. Alec picked up the tomato ketchup and began to vigorously squeeze its contents onto his plate. A large blob of sauce landed on the envelope. 'Sorry!'

Aunty Florence picked up the envelope, obviously annoyed.

She said nothing, but carefully and very slowly peeled it open, without tearing it, and began to read.

'It's from a friend.' She hastily slid it into her pocket. 'Let's get on with breakfast before it gets cold.'

Later in the day, in the company of Isabel, Aunty Florence looked at the letter from 'a friend'. They sat down at the kitchen table, as she read aloud:

My dearest Florence,

*I cannot apologise enough for letting you down recently. Sadly,
Roy had taken a turn for the worse; he was rushed into
hospital, and passed away two days later. Since then I have
been so busy. Roy had asked me to organise his funeral
service. I've yet to meet his son. I might wonder if he really
existed, apart from the fact that I have spoken to him on the
telephone. The service is on Thursday, just after lunch.
I know that you hadn't ever met Roy, and this is an awful
cheek, but would you consider coming to the funeral with me
to give me some support at this sad time? I probably shouldn't
be asking this, so feel free to say no. But I would like to see
you again.
With kindest regards,
Stan*

'My dear Isabel, I am an awful woman! Fancy doubting Stan.'

Isabel put a comforting arm around her. 'Are you going to
go with him?'

'I think I should. Oh, I would like to see Stan again.'

Isabel smiled. 'Karen and Alec should be in soon. Karen
has been schooling Henry. I can't wait to be able to ride Diana
again.'

As Isabel got up, Aunty Florence suddenly spoke. 'I have
my reasons for not giving all of you young people the money
to buy this centre, you know.'

'You don't have to explain,' Isabel said, gently. 'After all,
it's a lot of money.'

The door flew open. 'You should have seen Henry today!'
Karen announced. 'We were doing some great dressage
movements – shoulder in, half pass and even some counter
canter.' She paused. 'Have I interrupted something?'

Isabel and Aunty Florence exchanged glances, and the
older woman nodded.

'Aunty Florence is going to a funeral with Stan on
Thursday. It's his neighbour Roy – he died quite suddenly.'

'Oh! So do I sense romance in the air?'

Aunty Florence smiled almost coyly.

'Does that mean you'll be getting married and moving out of here soon?'

'Is that what you want?'

Karen frowned. 'No, I was kidding – you're family.' Her face broke into a smile. She walked over and gave her aunt a bear hug. 'Let's put the past behind us and make a fresh start. I'm glad you're going with Stan.'

For a moment, Isabel thought she saw a tear trickling down Aunty Florence's cheek. She almost made comment, but thought better of it. 'It seems like forever, waiting to ride Diana again. I can't wait to be able to do some dressage with her.'

'Not too long before you have that cast off, dear,' Aunty Florence told her.

'And then how long before my leg is strong enough for me to ride again?'

Karen shrugged her shoulders. 'If we can't raise enough money to buy this place, neither of us will be riding anything.'

Isabel frowned. 'We'll just find somewhere else, won't we?'

Fifteen

April

Aunty Florence had persuaded Isabel to go along to the funeral as well – for moral support. As the taxi sped round the windy country lanes, Isabel grinned.

'I don't want to play gooseberry today. You'll have to say if you two want to be left alone.'

Aunty Florence fanned herself with a hand. 'Is it me, or is it warm in here?'

Suddenly the taxi driver piped up, 'Turned cool today, don't you think?'

'Stan and I are just two friends who enjoy each other's company; nothing more.'

'Of course you are!'

'You're teasing me,' Aunty Florence observed.

Isabel smiled. Aunty Florence seemed relaxed and *ordinary*, somehow. And even though she was wearing one of her black dresses, she seemed younger, less prim. Perhaps it was the chunky blue necklace that Karen had lent her.

Isabel was glad that the taxi driver was using a satnav. Fortunately, they had been able to obtain the postcode for the church from Stan the day before. She looked anxiously at her phone. 'Will we be there in time?'

'Don't worry, young lady. We'll be there.'

'It's just that we don't want to arrive after the coffin has gone in.'

'I understand.'

Sure enough, they were fifteen minutes early. Stan was waiting for them.

'You look very smart, Stan,' Isabel commented.

'I'm not really a suit person,' he explained. 'I like something a little less formal.'

'Well you certainly scrub up well,' Aunty Florence added.

'I'll come and sit with you,' Stan explained. 'The son will walk behind the coffin and I believe there are some nephews coming.'

Isabel admired Stan's humility; after all, if he hadn't organised the service, there probably wouldn't have been one. And now he was standing back, because he recognised that it was the family's day.

'Let's sit in the middle somewhere,' Aunty Florence suggested.

'Whatever you say, Florence.'

Isabel noticed him give Karen's aunt a squeeze of the hand.

While she was waiting in the ambiance of the church, Isabel took the opportunity to say a prayer for those mourning the death of Roy, and also about the situation surrounding the future of the centre and the possibility of them all – including the horses and ponies – becoming homeless. 'Please help us, God,' she asked silently.

Aware that things had suddenly gone quiet, Isabel prepared to stand, nudging her two friends. 'The hearse has arrived.'

Sadly, the vicar had only been in the area for about eighteen months and Roy had been unable to get to church for at least three years. The young clergyman had done his best to find out as much as he could about the deceased, but still his approach to the service and references to Roy seemed impersonal to Isabel. Roy's son also spoke about his father with a vagueness that had developed through lack of contact over many years. He began a long list of thank yous: 'Thank you to the vicar, the organist, the funeral director, the hospital staff, the lady who had prepared the floral tributes... oh, and to Mrs Grey who prepared the refreshments.' But there was no reference to the good neighbour who had cared for and supported Roy for many years.

After the service, Stan politely and respectfully sat for a few minutes while the family followed the coffin into the graveyard.

'I would like to have a chat with Roy's son before he goes.'

'I expect he will want to see you to say a big thank you,' Isabel remarked.

'I don't want any fuss.'

'Fancy him not even mentioning all that you did for Roy,' Aunty Florence said, frowning. 'Why was that?'

'What's happened to Roy's son?' Stan whispered to the funeral director moments later.

'I'm afraid he had to leave straight after the service; a taxi was waiting for him.'

Isabel could see that Stan was trying to cover up his disappointment with a large smile. 'I understand, only… well, I guess it doesn't really matter.'

People began to disperse soon after the burial. Stan led the way into the church hall where there was an array of food laid out. There was a wide selection of assorted cold meats, pasta salads, potato salad, coleslaw, samosas, vol-au-vents, sushi and numerous gateaux and cheesecakes, and fruit juice to drink.

As Stan examined the spread he commented, 'Roy would have wanted something simple, but his son intervened in the arrangements. I just wanted tea, coffee, a few sandwiches and some homemade fruit cake.'

Aunty Florence put her arm round him affectionately. 'Never mind, Stan. You did your best for Roy. You've been a good friend to him.'

Stan smiled. 'Perhaps we could go up the road to the little coffee shop there.'

Over a mug of steaming hot filter coffee, the topic of conversation turned to the equestrian centre.

'It's kind of put an end to all our thoughts about setting up a breeding programme for quality coloured horses,' Isabel explained. 'I was thinking about having Diana put into foal to Henry. I probably won't be able to ride seriously for some time yet – but then I thought, how can we plan anything at the moment? The centre could be closed in a few months.'

Stan was deep in thought. 'Life is short. Reach out for your dreams; if you lose the centre, something else will open up for you. You'll find somewhere else.'

'Take Diana to the stallion as soon as she comes into season – do it, despite the uncertainly,' Aunty Florence added.

'But what if...'

Stan interrupted, 'You can't live your whole life thinking, what if? You know how much I love coloured horses, and that I really want to be included in your plans to breed quality coloured horses and ponies for competition. We have to be positive!'

Aunty Florence suddenly looked uncomfortable. 'I did have my reasons for not giving the money. I would...'

'That's all right,' Isabel consoled her. 'We shouldn't have assumed.'

'But you do need to come up with some alternative ideas of how you could raise the money,' Stan reasoned.

Isabel drank the rest of her coffee. 'I'm going to have a look round the shops for half an hour, and leave you two to have a chat on your own. I'll meet you back at the taxi rank at four.' She picked up her crutches. 'See you later.'

While Isabel stood at the window of a jeweller's shop, looking at a tray of very expensive earrings, suddenly she was aware of having company.

'Well, well, if it isn't the girl with the crutches again.'

She swung round to see the same two very large men who had visited the centre on behalf of Crawford-Smith. 'What do you want?'

The bald one commented, 'Now, is that any way to greet old friends?'

'Mr Crawford-Smith is getting very impatient now. He's not nice when he gets angry,' the second man warned.

They turned. Isabel could see them standing head and shoulders above everyone else as they walked up the crowded street. She felt very vulnerable, wondering if this had been a coincidental meeting; maybe she had been followed. She was trembling when she met up with the others.

'You look as if you've seen a ghost! What is it, dear?' Aunty Florence asked, concerned.

Isabel relayed what had happened. 'They're probably watching us now. Perhaps we should just give up and let Crawford-Smith have the property.'

Stan gently took hold of Isabel's right hand. 'Reach out for your dreams and don't let ignorant bullies spoil it for you.'

'But what if…'

'What did I say about the what ifs?'

The journey home seemed a long one. Not much was said between the two passengers. Isabel knew that Aunty Florence wished she could do more to help. And Isabel herself struggled to grasp the idea of following her dreams, especially with facing the bullies and the what ifs.

On their arrival home, Isabel pointed to an unfamiliar car parked in front of the house. It was unusual for clients to park there.

'It looks like a rental car,' Isabel commented.

'Who do you know that would be renting a car?'

Isabel scrambled out, intrigued by the vehicle, while Aunty Florence settled the bill.

The back door flew open, and Basil ran out with the labradoodle puppy in hot pursuit.

'Isabel!'

An older woman with black frizzy hair stood in the doorway.

'Mum!'

Isabel's mum frowned as she sipped her tea. 'I came on my own, on the train and then picked up a hire car. I was hoping you might put me up for a couple of days.'

There were no hugs or kisses. Isabel knew there was too much healing that needed to take place for that to happen just yet.

'Mum, it's so good to see you. I'm so sorry Dad couldn't be here too.'

'Yes, well.' Her mother put her mug down on the kitchen table, frowning. 'You know how he feels. He's very hurt. All that money he paid on giving you a good education at that amazing private school. It had such a good reputation!'

Isabel felt exasperated. 'Why can't you just be happy for me to work with horses, following my dream?'

Isabel's mother had that look of disapproval that Isabel had become so familiar with.

'Let's face it; you'll never earn a proper living from taking out rides across the heath on a few decrepit old horses and ponies.'

Isabel felt deflated. 'Nothing has changed, has it, Mum?'

Aunty Florence walked into the kitchen and, without being invited, sat down at the table. 'Ah! So this is your mother, Isabel? You must be tired from travelling, Mrs...'

'Price,' came the cold reply.

'You're tired from travelling, Mrs Price. Perhaps this is not the time to be sorting out issues from the past.'

Karen popped her head round the door. 'I'll get the back bedroom ready for you, if you'd like to get your things sorted out, Mrs Price. I'll show you the room, then help you get your bags.'

Isabel's mother said nothing, but swept out of the room, following Karen.

'Dinner will be at seven!' Aunty Florence called after the visitor.

'She never fails to make me feel guilty and small – very small,' Isabel sighed.

Aunty Florence put her arm round her. 'She's nothing but a bully.'

'You wait until you meet my dad.' Isabel hesitated. 'Although that doesn't seem likely to happen.'

Karen returned. 'That was a nice surprise to have a visit from your mum, eh? I'm doing a roast for dinner. Lucky I had a joint in the fridge.' She looked at Isabel. 'Look, now's your chance to put the past behind you. She's your mum. Hug and make up.'

Isabel glanced at Aunty Florence. 'If only it were as easy as that.'

'Your father and I had such great hopes for you, Isabel.'

It was a beautifully prepared dinner, but Isabel was quickly losing her appetite.

'Don't pick at your food dear,' Isabel's mother scolded. 'You know how much that kind of thing annoys me.'

Karen intervened. 'What are your plans for Diana, Isabel?'

She thought for a moment before replying. 'I would like to do some dressage and show jumping competitions, but I suppose, realistically, it might be best to breed a foal from her – to give my leg time to heal up properly.'

'Would you cover her with Henry?'

Mrs Price interrupted. 'Must we talk about such things at the dinner table, Isabel? Look, it's not too late to go to college and train for a proper job.'

'This *is* a proper job.'

'If you stay in the world of horses, you'll only end up failing again, just like you did in your dancing when you were young!'

'But Mum, I damaged a tendon in my leg. That was why I stopped dancing. It wasn't my fault.'

Aunty Florence intervened. 'I admire the girls for having a go. You're right. It's not easy making a living in the equestrian world, but why shouldn't they try to follow their dreams? They could so easily have given up,' Aunty Florence went on, 'especially when all this business with Crawford-Smith started…' She stopped, realising that maybe she had said too much.

'What's that?' Isabel's mother demanded.

'Oh, nothing!'

'Isabel?'

Isabel sighed. 'Our landlord died suddenly. The centre is due to go to auction in August, unless we can raise the money ourselves to buy it. We could lose it if we can't raise more than £500,000 in the next few weeks. Crawford-Smith is a ruthless property developer who wants to buy it and build a huge holiday complex.'

Isabel's mother smiled. 'Well, then, sweetheart: that proves my point.' At that moment, Stan the labradoodle rushed in and seemed to make a beeline for Isabel's mum. 'Oh! I can't abide dogs that jump up. Get down!'

'Get down, Stan!' shouted Karen.

'Stan?' Mrs Price seemed bewildered as the puppy jumped up and began to try to lick her face. Karen dragged him off.

'I'm so sorry. He's not allowed in the dining room. My husband's away working, but if he was here, he'd…'

'Colin!' Aunty Florence sat back. 'I've called him Colin again. It would be too complicated having two Stans around.'

Mrs Price blinked a few times.

The rest of the meal passed in silence.

The girls were up early the next morning; they were expecting two visiting mares to arrive to be covered by Henry. So as well as the normal stable yard routine, there were lessons to take and two stables to get ready for the visitors, who were due to arrive at about half past two.

Isabel was doing her best to spread shavings on the floor of one of the stables – not easy with her leg in plaster – as her friend tied up a hay net. 'Are you excited?'

Karen looked a little bewildered. 'What?'

'Can't you rustle up a little more enthusiasm?'

Karen turned round to face her. 'I can't feel enthusiastic about anything at the moment.'

Isabel leaned on her fork.

Karen mumbled, 'I suppose we need to stay positive.'

'I'm still praying about the situation.'

Karen shrugged. 'OK. Keep praying. It could work. You never know!'

Isabel's mother's visit seemed to pass quite quickly, but it was an awkward time for Isabel, who tried to keep out of her mother's way as much as possible.

'What are we going to do today?' Isabel's mother asked, on her last day. 'I've hardly seen you. You're always so busy. I've just been stuck here, in this farmhouse...'

'We did go shopping, Mum.'

'Oh yes. No decent shops, of course.'

Isabel took a deep breath. 'What about going somewhere we can sit and have a really long chat?'

They went for a drive round the coast, with a stop for lunch. But the 'chat' was just about the view, the coastline (Mrs Price was not impressed) and the food – which wasn't as good as Mrs Price was expecting.

As Isabel said her goodbyes the next day, there was still no fond embrace with her mother.

'Will I see you again?' Isabel ventured.

'I expect so.' Her mother suddenly planted a kiss on her daughter's cheek, but said no more.

Sixteen

As Isabel hobbled across the yard to break the good news to Diana – that she was soon going to become a mum, hopefully – her eye caught something lying on the ground, not very far from the back door. She nearly missed it; it had a jet-black cover and for a moment she didn't know what it was. Just a bit of rubbish? She bent down and to her surprise found it was a book. An old diary!

'Whoever...? What good would this be to anyone?'

There were no identifying marks on it. The little book seemed to fall open by itself at 24th July. She read:

> *I've decided. I'm leaving tonight. I haven't told anyone here yet. I cannot trust anyone. I cannot stand it any more... I've booked a taxi to pick me up at 10.30, outside the bowling alley. I can't wait.*

Isabel turned the page, expecting to find its continuation. But there was no more. Something must have disturbed the writer, or else the abrupt ending was a sign of his or her great hurry to escape. Anxious to discover who the writer was, she looked back to 3rd March:

> *I am feeling pleased with myself today. The matter that has been causing me much concern has now been dealt with. I am feeling safe and secure in that knowledge.*

Hurriedly flicking pages, Isabel arrived at 10th March:

> *I am planning my future. There are lots of things I'd like to do. I have always wanted to go up in a hot-air balloon and buy a red 1950s-style motorcycle.*

Isabel spotted Karen inside Henry's stable.

'Who do we know that would like to go up in a hot air balloon and own a red 1950s-style motorcycle?'

Karen stuck her head over the half-door. 'My darling husband would! He'd love to go up in a hot-air balloon, and he's always dreamed of having a red motorcycle – a classic, fifties-style thumper! Men are all big kids at heart. Why?'

'Oh, it doesn't matter.'

Isabel's thoughts turned to Ben, who was still away at a conference. Perhaps he'd dropped this diary in his rush to leave. But why would Ben keep an old diary? Perhaps he'd thrown it away and somehow it had finished up dumped by the stable door. The pages were damp. It had clearly been there for a little while.

She was suddenly concerned that he might be harbouring some tragic secret.

Isabel demonstrated considerable fleetness of movement on crutches as she escaped further questions. She went into Diana's stable, fondled the mare's nose affectionately, and then perched herself in the corner. Surrounded by the aroma of fresh hay, Isabel began to turn some more pages:

> *29th May*
> *Received shock news in the post, this morning – it changes everything! I was confident that things had been sorted out. Can't write any more at the moment, my mind is spinning. I'll go out for a walk to clear it.*
>
> *14th July*
> *Serious repercussions from news of 29th May.*
>
> *23rd July*
> *Not sure whether to stay and face the music, or run. I have a cousin in South Africa. If I could get there I could make a fresh start. Leave the past behind.*

Isabel was shocked. Could Ben really have reached a point of such desperation and considered leaving Karen, to go and live with a cousin in South Africa? And was it something he was still thinking about? Would he leave her if they lost the centre?

Diana neighed in a knowing sort of way, and nuzzled Isabel's shoulder affectionately. Isabel toyed with whether or not to talk to Karen about it – or Ben, who was due home tomorrow. She decided to put the diary somewhere safe for a few days or so, until she'd maybe had a word with him. Grasping the little book carefully with the fingertips of her right hand, simultaneously holding the handle of a crutch, she hurried across the yard trying not to be spotted by Karen.

Isabel breathed a sigh of relief as she closed the back door behind her. 'Now to find a safe hiding place.' She hid it in her sock drawer.

Over dinner that evening, she said, 'I've got to go to the hospital tomorrow, hopefully to have the plaster removed. The taxi is coming at half past one.'

'I'll come with you,' Aunty Florence volunteered. 'Maybe we could call in and say hello to Stan.'

That night, Isabel prayed.

> *Hi God. Please don't let it hurt when they take the plaster cast off… and don't let them put another one on in its place. I know it didn't hurt last time, but I still worry.*

She paused thoughtfully for a few moments before concluding:

> *I feel a bit if a wimp, but I know You're concerned about the small things that worry us, as well as the big worldwide issues! And please – give me wisdom over what to say to Ben, and don't let him leave Karen. Amen.*

The next day, Isabel felt nervous as she watched the cutter moving swiftly through the plaster, getting closer and closer to her skin.

'It's OK, love, no need to panic!' The technician winked at her.

Isabel could feel the trickle of sweat running down her back. She wasn't sure if it was entirely the fear of the little machine or the apprehension of being able to use her leg once again. Rumour had it that it was not uncommon for people to go home and accidentally re-break limbs at such a time.

'Nearly there now, love.' The technician began to ease the two halves of the plaster cast apart.

'It'll seem strange not having the plaster on any more,' she commented. 'I've grown used to life with a cast on my leg.'

The technician laughed. 'All done – good as new. Well, nearly!'

Isabel thanked the technician and set off to find Aunty Florence, who had been trying to phone Stan to make arrangements to meet him for coffee in town.

'He's agreed to meet us at quarter past four,' Aunty Florence confirmed.

'It'll be really good to see Stan again,' Isabel said as they got out of the taxi, being very tentative about placing weight on her leg once again.

Aunty Florence gazed into space. 'Dear, sweet Stan.'

Stan was already waiting at the table when his two guests arrived. He jumped up and gave Isabel a fond peck on the cheek before turning to her companion.

'Florence, it's so good to see you again!' He flung his good arm around her, and seemed reluctant to let her go.

A young waitress interrupted the embrace. 'What can I get you?'

Stan smiled, looking a little embarrassed. 'Sorry!'

'We've got a special offer price for a fruit scone and a regular coffee.'

'That'll do,' Aunty Florence replied.

The young waitress sauntered off to the kitchen.

'How's the leg?' Stan asked, letting go of Aunty Florence, somewhat reluctantly, Isabel thought.

She sat down very carefully. 'It feels a bit weak, and my ankle is very stiff. But it's early days yet. They've let me keep the crutches for a while longer.'

'Give it time. You'll be surprised how quickly it'll get back to normal,' he reassured her. He rubbed his arm. 'I shall be glad to get my plaster cast off. It's not healing as quickly as they'd hoped.'

The waitress returned unenthusiastically. 'We've only got two fruit scones left, so I've brought a cheese scone as well.'

Aunty Florence moved to complain, but Stan put his hand gently over hers. 'It's all right. I prefer savoury, my dear.'

Aunty Florence appeared to mellow before Isabel's eyes. 'If you're sure?'

The topic of conversation soon turned to Diana.

'So have you decided what to do with Diana while your leg is still healing?' Stan asked.

Isabel grinned. 'I'm going to put her into foal.'

Aunty Florence's mind had apparently gone off on a tangent. 'Perhaps there's a legal loophole regarding the centre.'

Stan frowned as he buttered his scone. 'It's worth a try. Trouble is, solicitors are expensive.'

'Not if one owes you a favour,' Isabel commented thoughtfully. 'And I know just the person.'

She explained about the wallet that she had found and returned, containing a treasured ring. 'Archie's a retired solicitor. He offered free legal advice if we ever need it. I've got his business card at home.'

'Then give him a call.'

'That's plan A,' Stan said, 'but we really need a plan B as well.'

Isabel grinned. 'I think I might have a plan B already.'

The young waitress walked towards them, dragging an empty tea trolley. 'We're closing in five minutes.'

Isabel picked up her bag. 'We'd better go. I'll announce plan B after I've had a chance to get something down on paper.'

Seventeen

That evening, everyone sat around the kitchen table, each clasping a mug of hot chocolate.

'We're waiting,' Aunty Florence said with apparent impatience. 'If plan A is contacting Archie to see if he can find a legal loophole, what is plan B?'

'Come on! It's been a long day, and I want to go to bed,' Karen said as she yawned loudly.

Ben and Alec sipped their hot chocolate. Colin barked and wagged his tail excitedly, almost as if he too were waiting with bated breath. Isabel opened a small notebook and looked at it thoughtfully.

'Plan B is to see if we could somehow raise enough money from people who'd support us, and then get a mortgage too. We could buy the property between us.'

Ben smiled. 'Great! But how much are you planning to raise? And more to the point, how are you planning to raise it?'

'I thought about contacting the press, making it into a sob story. Maybe someone would be prepared to give us an interest-free loan or something.'

'You mean, enough to put down a deposit on the property and to be able to get an affordable mortgage for the rest?'

Karen sighed. 'Surely we'd have to raise at least two-thirds of the money to be able to afford a mortgage for the balance?'

'Maybe the newspaper would like a story,' Alec suggested. 'And then someone might come up with the money, like Isabel said.'

'There's a reporter for a local paper who rides horses. I don't know her personally. She's a friend of a friend,' Karen said, thoughtfully. 'I could give her a ring.'

Ben was tapping away at the calculator on his phone. 'Hmm. Don't get your hopes up. Plan B may not even be a possibility.'

Ben, Karen and Aunty Florence went off to bed, leaving Alec and Isabel still sitting at the kitchen table.

Isabel moved closer to the range, holding her hands out to feel the warmth. 'Just listen to that dog snoring.'

Colin was fast asleep, on his bed in the corner.

'Isabel, can I ask you something?' Alec sounded tentative and Isabel glanced at him. 'You believe in God. Well, if God is a God of love, why do bad things happen?' He hesitated. 'Like us losing Henry's Stud and Equestrian Centre.'

Isabel smiled. 'God doesn't make bad things happen, but sometimes He allows bad things to happen, for a purpose.'

'So what's the purpose in us losing this place?'

'We haven't lost anything yet.'

Alec nodded. 'True!'

The next morning, Isabel rang Archie.

'Do you remember me? I found your wallet.'

'Of course I do! The equestrian centre. How are you?'

'Well, you know you offered to help, if I needed it? I'd really like to ask your advice. Perhaps we could meet for a coffee some time?'

Archie sounded only too pleased to be of help. 'I meant what I said about free legal advice. How would tomorrow morning suit? I can come over to the centre at about half past ten.'

Isabel sighed with relief. 'That would be wonderful.'

At that moment, Karen came into the tack room.

'Have you called the reporter?' Isabel asked. 'How did it go?'

'Answering machine: "I am sorry, but I am out of the office at the moment, please leave a message after the tone." You know how much I hate those things. I'll phone again this afternoon, then I'll send a covering email with a few details about the centre.'

The next day Archie arrived in his little black classic car, greeted the ladies with a kiss on the hand, and finally sat down to a cup of coffee with three teaspoons of sugar in it.

'Now, what's this all about?'

'We're going to lose the equestrian centre!' Karen said dramatically. 'The owner has died and left instructions that we should be given the opportunity to buy within a set period of time. If we're not able to raise the funds, then it'll go to auction.'

'We only have a short time left to raise the money,' Aunty Florence added, rather bluntly.

Ben commented, 'And we don't have much chance of raising that kind of money.'

'Is there some kind of small print that we might be able to take advantage of?' Aunty Florence asked.

Archie shook his head. 'From what you have said, the bequest of the deceased was quite specific. I have no reason to believe that there would be any discrepancies. Besides, legal battles can be long-winded and very expensive. I wouldn't advise you to go down that route even if we could find a loophole.' He took out his wallet and, digging deep, brought out the ring that had belonged to his late wife. For what seemed like ages, he lovingly rolled it around in his hand. 'I don't think I can sell this and let you use the money for the centre as an interest-free loan.' He paused and glanced at Isabel. 'I was impressed with your honesty, and I would love to help you more. But the ring means too much to me. I'm sorry!'

'Oh, Archie,' Isabel cried, taken aback by the generosity of such a thought, 'we couldn't let you do that anyway. You hardly know us.'

'It's very kind of you to even consider that,' Ben told him, 'but it wouldn't be anywhere close to being enough to get us out of trouble – but thank you, anyway. We need more than £500,000.'

'That much?' Archie put the ring back into his wallet with some obvious relief.

'It's our plan B. Plan A, the loophole, isn't going to work, obviously,' Isabel said sadly.

'So we need to raise the bulk of the money from gifts or long-term investors. We haven't got sufficient income to pay back a large mortgage,' Ben explained.

Archie smiled. 'I wish I could help.' He got up to go. 'I wish you every success in raising the money.'

As Isabel rose to take Archie to the door, the house phone rang.

Karen picked it up. 'Hi, Sue. Thanks for ringing back.'

'Here goes,' Karen announced to the others a few days later. 'The beginning of plan B.'

'Good for you, darling. It's a start,' Ben encouraged, as he got into his car. 'I'll be home about seven.'

Isabel put her hand up for a high five. 'Well done, Karen.'

As Ben drove out of the yard, he left Karen and Isabel leaning up against the gate of the ponies' meadow. Suddenly, Isabel felt something nudging her in the back. She turned round to see Max, one of the older ponies.

'Sorry, boy, I've got nothing for you!' She reached over the gate and rubbed the pony's nose.

At that moment a large, luxurious, silver metallic 4x4 purred effortlessly in to the yard.

'This must be Sue,' Karen commented, as she tried to subtly peer through the tinted windows. 'Be on your best behaviour.'

The door opened slowly, and after changing her footwear, a short, slightly rotund woman climbed out of the vehicle. Isabel thought she looked like a combination of middle-aged business executive and someone from the hunting fraternity. A very smart pin-striped skirt and jacket were partly covered by a quilted waistcoat and she was wearing green Wellington boots. Before closing the door, she reached into the car for a small, black leather briefcase.

Karen walked over to introduce herself. 'Hi, I'm Karen.' After shaking hands, she pointed to Isabel. 'And this is one of my employees, Isabel. We both have an interest in the centre and its future.'

Karen sensed that perhaps Sue would like to conduct the initial meeting inside. 'Do come into the house. I'll make some coffee.'

Aunty Florence joined them, and they sat around the dining room table. Sue took a letter out of her briefcase. 'I have a copy of the letter that you emailed to me, Karen. What exactly are you hoping I can do for you?'

'I know you're interested in horses, and often write horsy features in your newspaper. We wondered if you could give us some publicity that might help our plight.'

Sue sipped her coffee. 'Well, as you will appreciate, I receive a lot of communications from different individuals and organisations wanting this kind of help. I know you outlined something of the story in your letter. But what's different about your situation that warrants me doing a feature on this place?'

There was a long pause as everyone thought how they could justify a feature in the newspaper.

Isabel was the one to break the silence. 'There are too many big organisations bulldozing people out of their homes and livelihoods.'

Sue nodded.

'If our landlord hadn't died suddenly, we wouldn't have been in this mess,' Karen added.

'My niece is just trying to make an honest living,' Aunty Florence pointed out.

Sue smiled. 'I know, it can be very hard sometimes. Everything can seem to be against you. I was interviewing a dairy farmer who had gone out of business, last week – tragic story. They'd been in the trade for three generations.'

'We're trying to develop a programme for breeding quality coloured horses for competition use. We've got our own 17hh Hanoverian stallion and the first of our quality coloured broodmares, a 16.1hh, three-quarter thoroughbred, skewbald mare that we're going to cover as soon as we can. We want to see quality coloured horses at the top of show jumping, dressage and cross country. So many people frown on them as second best. We want an end to the stigma of riding a skewbald or piebald horse or pony in competition,' Isabel added with passion.

'I see! Now, that's something that could make news, especially if you could breed a really good-quality coloured stallion.' Sue paused. 'Let's go outside and have a look round the yard. And maybe, later on, I could get changed and have a ride on this stallion of yours?'

Isabel sensed her friend's reluctance, but they all knew that this was someone who might be the enablement of plan B.

'Of course. I'll ask Alec to get him ready.'

As they walked round the yard, Sue explained, 'I do have a contact in the horse trade – saddlery, clothing, jumps – you know the kind of thing. I don't know if there would be any cash involved, but he would probably be prepared to offer sponsorship in terms of equipment, if this stallion of yours is any good.'

'That sounds great, but it's more important to get the money to stay open at the moment,' Karen replied.

'Understood! But I'm sure you wouldn't turn down a really nice dressage saddle, quality rugs, best quality leather bridle… you know!'

'I guess not. But if we don't find the money to stay open, saddles and rugs won't be much help.'

'If we can put together a really good article, including a nice picture of your skewbald mare, something about the discrimination against coloured horses found in some riding circles, your plans to breed a special kind of coloured horse specifically aimed at the world of top competition – and then the potential loss of premises...' Sue pondered. 'Some philanthropist might come out of the woodwork.'

'Really?' Isabel responded, excitedly.

'Well, it's a possibility.'

'So you'll definitely do an article, then?'

'It's a definite possibility.'

'This is Diana, my skewbald mare,' Isabel proudly announced as they passed her stable.

At the sound of Isabel's voice, the mare's head shot out over the door. Sue looked into the stable.

'She's something quite special, isn't she?' the journalist commented. 'Cover her with a really nice thoroughbred stallion and, if it's a coloured colt, you could end up with a fantastic stallion.'

Karen seemed a little put out. 'I think Henry is ready for you to ride now. I know you'll love him.'

'I'll need to get my riding clothes from the car and change somewhere first.'

After Sue had grabbed a large bag from the car, Karen directed her to the family bathroom. 'We'll wait for you in the kitchen.'

As they waited, Karen seemed to be on edge. 'I know that Diana is a beautiful mare, and I can understand the logic of trying to produce a quality coloured stallion of a different bloodline from Henry's, but...'

'Not now, Karen,' Isabel whispered. 'We have to think about the centre.'

'I think I'll need the mounting block,' Sue concluded, when Henry was led out into the yard for her. 'I hope he's not one of these stallions that never really concentrates on school work.'

'Of course he's not,' Karen replied, quickly.

It soon became clear that Sue was a competent horsewoman as she put Henry through his paces, doing some dressage movements including shoulder in, half pass, counter canter and a couple of flying changes. The girls, leaning on the gate, watched in surprise.

'What do you think of him?' Karen called. 'Is he what you expected?'

Sue nodded, and walked the horse over to the gate. 'I have to admit that I'm not a particular lover of Hanoverians – I prefer thoroughbreds – but, having said that, he rides very well.' She looked at Isabel. 'But I still think you should put your mare to a thoroughbred stallion.'

As the three women wandered back towards Sue's car, Sue turned to Isabel and Karen. 'I'll prepare an article in the next week or two. In the meantime, I'll give you details of the contact I told you about earlier – the one who might be able to offer some kind of sponsorship deal.' She scribbled down his name and details of a company website, when they reached the car. 'Give him a call and mention my name.'

Karen took the slip of paper. 'Thank you. I do appreciate this.'

Sue turned to Isabel and handed her a small stud card. 'Go and have a look at this stallion. I think you'll be impressed. He'd really suit your mare.' With that, she climbed into her 4x4 and slammed the door shut. The car window opened effortlessly and without any sound. 'I'll be in touch!'

The engine roared into life, and moments later the vehicle disappeared up the road, in a cloud of dust.

At that moment, Aunty Florence came out from the house. 'Has she gone?'

Karen nodded, but Isabel's mind was on other things.

'*Standing at Manor Farm Stud. Thunder Bay, 16.3hh Bay Thoroughbred Stallion,*' Isabel read out. There was a small photograph of the horse on the reverse side, and contact details. 'He looks beautiful.'

'How did it all go?' Aunty Florence asked as they went in to the kitchen.

Karen frowned, appearing to still be a little disgruntled. 'I'm not sure how interested she was in the centre. All she kept on about was Isabel's mare being put in foal to a thoroughbred stallion.'

'That's not true!' Isabel protested. 'I thought it was all very positive. She's going to write an article about the centre, and she's given Karen someone to contact about sponsoring Henry.'

Karen relented. 'OK, so I was a bit peeved that she obviously liked Diana better than Henry, but she was quite positive.'

'What are we waiting for, then?' Isabel said excitedly. 'Let's have a look at that website address she gave you.'

The three women scurried into the dining room where Karen's laptop sat on the table. Moments later the website opened up, showing a display of brightly coloured show jumps and miscellaneous horse accessories.

'They seem to sell everything a horse owner might need,' Isabel commented. 'Even horseboxes and trailers!'

Karen eagerly searched the website.

'Take a look at that amazing dressage saddle,' she said. 'I need to sit down with Ben and sort out a formal letter to these people to see if we can get sponsorship for Henry.'

The house phone began to ring. Isabel jumped up to answer it. It was an enquiry about riding lessons. Suddenly, she was brought back down to earth with the realisation that – first and foremost – they had a stud farm and riding school to run.

Over dinner that night, Ben looked ill at ease. 'I'm concerned that Crawford-Smith isn't going to be giving up without a fight.'

Karen shrugged. 'We've heard nothing from him lately.'

'Yes, but with someone like him, no news is probably not good news,' Isabel commented.

'I think she's right,' Ben agreed, as he picked at his dinner.

'Do you know something?' Karen demanded.

Ben glanced round at the others, looking very evasive.

'Well,' he explained, 'it's like this.' He hesitated. 'I've spoken to one or two of the neighbours. It would appear that Crawford-Smith has been asking around, wanting to buy them out. Some of them have already agreed to sell, in principle.'

'Oh, great.' Karen leaned back in her seat.

'The more interested they are in selling, the more determined he's going to be to get this place,' Isabel said, quietly. She took a deep breath. 'You know what? I'm really going to pray about the centre. I think we *all* need to say a prayer tonight.' And as she glanced at Ben, she thought about the diary. Should she tackle him about it or not?

Eighteen

'Are you sure we're on the right road?' Karen asked anxiously.

Aunty Florence was staring at Karen's phone. 'According to this we should come to a T-junction in about two miles, where we turn left.'

Isabel had reluctantly agreed to drive Karen's shiny new car – for fear of scratching it.

'How does it feel to be behind the wheel again?' Karen asked.

'I'm OK. I'm taking it steady,' Isabel replied. She pulled back the switch to clean the windscreen. There was a faint aroma of detergent. 'I hate all these flies that get stuck on the glass.'

Having left the main road two or three miles back, they were plunged into the depths of the south Norfolk countryside.

'Would you believe it?' Isabel commented. 'There's not a house to be seen.'

Everywhere was beginning to look green: the crops, the trees, and even the grass verge and hedgerow. The sound of birdsong could be heard through the open car window. The breeze ruffled Isabel's hair. She brushed it back, away from her face.

'It's impossible to be sad or negative on a day like today,' she announced. 'Everywhere looks, sounds and smells so beautiful. Spring is well and truly here now.'

'Don't kid yourself. The countryside smell is just the screen wash,' Karen muttered.

'Why must you always be so…'

'So practical, the one who writes the cheques each month to pay the bills and is worried sick about what's going to happen to us when the bailiffs come round? Well, one of us has to be like that!'

'Girls!' Aunty Florence intervened. 'We're all worried about the future! Let's not argue.'

But Isabel spoke again. 'So what happens when we allow them to quash our hopes and dreams, Karen? What then?'

'Who are *they*?'

'*They* are the Crawford-Smiths of this world, the hierarchy, bureaucracy, those huge faceless companies, bullies who have no scruples about how they use their power! I don't know. Why should we stand to one side and allow people like that to crush the dreams we hope for and work for?'

Karen stared at her. 'So what's your point?'

'We're going to look at a thoroughbred stallion, to put Diana in foal to, in the hope that she will produce a top-quality skewbald colt – suitable to keep as a stallion – in order to develop a breeding programme to produce quality coloured event horses. The reason we're doing that, despite the fact that we may lose the yard, is that we're not going to give in to the bullies. We're not going to give up our dream, our hopes.'

Aunty Florence clapped her hands. 'Good for you, Isabel.'

Karen said nothing.

'And we need to stand up for coloured horses – they've been ostracised long enough.' Isabel's voice was wavering. 'We need to show people that coloured horses can be just as good as any other horses.'

'Turn left here!' Aunty Florence called out.

Isabel slowed down. 'We should be able to see a large white farm gate soon – on the right, with a sign on it saying "Manor Farm Stud".'

Sure enough, as the car pulled into the farmyard they could see the bay thoroughbred stallion's head out over the door of the stable.

'There he is,' Isabel squealed. 'Thunder Bay.'

'Are you positive that you're doing the right thing, Isabel?' her friend asked.

'Not until I've seen him in the flesh and sussed out his temperament. I've already studied his breeding and watched videos of his and his parents' performance on the internet – both in dressage and show jumping.'

A well-built man of about thirty-five was walking towards them with a bridle hanging over his shoulder. 'Hello, I'm Matthew Gibson. Pleased to meet you.'

After the introductions, Matthew led the three women across to the stable. Isabel watched as he went in, to see how the horse behaved in the stable.

'I'll just put his bridle on, and then I'll bring him out.' He glanced at them. 'You obviously found your way OK.'

As the big stallion pranced out into the yard, snorting loudly, Isabel brushed back her long curly hair, a grin on her face. 'Wow, he's got such presence.'

Aunty Florence stepped back nervously. 'He's a bit excitable!'

'Shall I trot him across the yard?' Mathew asked.

Isabel nodded. 'Yes, please.'

Thunder Bay trotted enthusiastically across the yard and back. Isabel watched in amazement.

'Well, what do you think?' Mathew asked.

'He moves beautifully!' Isabel smiled. 'Is he OK to handle?'

Matthew reasoned. 'You've seen him in the stable, and led in hand...' He went round picking up each of the big horse's hooves. '... and now you've seen him lift his feet.'

Isabel felt her heart skip a beat as she visualised what Diana's offspring would be like. But...

'What do you think, Karen?'

Her friend sighed. 'OK. I suppose he is quite impressive,' she admitted.

Isabel turned to Matthew, decisively. 'When can I bring Diana over?'

'I'm still having doubts about the future,' Karen muttered. 'I don't know how you can be so confident.'

'Come on,' Isabel urged. 'Be excited with me.'

'OK. I'll try.'

Matthew led the stallion back into his stable. 'Come into the house for a hot drink, and I'll give you details about cost and terms and conditions.'

The three women followed Matthew into the huge farmhouse kitchen. It looked as if it had been recently fitted out in a traditional style. Isabel took a deep breath, inhaling the aroma of fresh herbs.

A woman was there, elegant, with long blonde hair. Isabel felt a little intimidated by how glamorous she looked. Her accent suggested she was from a privileged upbringing.

'Pleased to meet you all. I'm Emma. What did you think of Thunder Bay, then?'

Isabel grinned. 'We are very impressed!'

Matthew indicated his guests to sit down on a restored oak church pew, as he filled the kettle and stood it on the range.

Emma carefully arranged five bone china cups and saucers and some very fancy teaspoons onto a silver tea tray, together with a small jug of milk and a bowl of sugar cubes. 'Have you come far?'

Karen shook her head. 'Not too far. We live on the north Norfolk coast.'

While the kettle was boiling, Matthew produced a glossy, coloured brochure from a drawer and handed it to Isabel. 'All the costs and terms and conditions are in there. When your mare is ready to cover, give us a call and we'll arrange for you to bring her over.'

'Presumably you'll keep her here for a few days,' Isabel said.

Matthew poured the hot water into the teapot. 'We'll keep the mare as long as you want us to. The livery fees are in the brochure. Some people like to leave the mares with us until we're pretty sure they're in foal.'

Moments later, tea strainer in hand, Matthew carefully began to pour the tea. In the meantime, Isabel glanced at the brochure.

'It's very expensive,' she whispered to Karen. 'But I guess you get what you pay for. Thankfully the money that my grandmother left me will cover it.'

Matthew suddenly looked up. Isabel hoped that he hadn't caught her comment. She smiled.

'Nothing like a nice cup of tea in a proper cup and saucer.' But then she thought that had probably sounded rather patronising and, in an attempt not to dig herself into a deeper hole, decided to keep quiet.

On their way home, Karen sniggered. 'Nothing like a nice cup of tea in a proper cup and saucer!' she said mischievously. 'Whatever did they think of you?'

'I like a proper cup and saucer,' Isabel said in her defence. 'The tea tastes better.'

'It was a whole different era,' Aunty Florence commented. 'I was surprised they didn't make cucumber sandwiches with the crusts cut off.'

They all laughed.

'Anyway, the point is this,' Isabel said emphatically, as she slowed the car down for a junction, 'I've decided to take Diana to Thunder Bay – no disrespect to Henry. He really is a lovely horse, and if Diana breeds a good coloured colt that we decide to keep as a stallion, it's another bloodline.'

'True,' Karen agreed.

'You're definitely going to put Diana in foal, despite the uncertainty?' Aunty Florence queried.

'Definitely!'

Isabel was reminded of Stan's quiet decisiveness. She admired his determination to do the right thing.

Karen perused the brochure. 'He is certainly a lovely horse, and by all accounts from some very good stock. I'm sure his offspring will be a credit to the centre – whether it's a filly or a colt.' There followed a few moments' silence, broken by Karen. 'So are you still praying about the centre then, Isabel?'

'Of course!'

Aunty Florence said in a soft voice. 'That's nice, dear.'

'It might be nice, Aunty Florence,' Karen commented, 'but nothing seems to be happening yet.'

Isabel didn't reply.

Isabel, Karen and Aunty Florence arrived home to be greeted by Stan.

'This is a pleasant surprise!' Aunty Florence exclaimed.

Stan grinned, holding up his arm. 'I managed to get a lift over here to tell you that I had my plaster removed today. I should be driving myself again soon. I didn't realise you'd be out gallivanting!'

'Not exactly gallivanting,' Karen replied, a little defensively.

'I'm only kidding.'

'I'm sorry. It's just rather a difficult time.'

'That's OK. It must be really hard for you to stay positive, with everything that's going on.'

Isabel grabbed Stan's hand. 'Anyway, come on inside.'

Later, Stan handed a large envelope to Aunty Florence. 'I bought this voucher at an auction in aid of the church last night. I thought you might enjoy it.'

Excitedly, Aunty Florence ripped the large envelope open. 'Oh, Stan! That sounds absolutely wonderful! When can we go?'

Nineteen

'What a lovely surprise this is, Stan. How sweet you are!' Florence exclaimed, as they both floated along in the hot-air balloon. 'It's always been one of my dreams – that and owning a red thumper.'

'I wasn't sure if you'd like it or not, Florence.'

'Oh look – there are some deer on that field down below. Aren't they beautiful?'

Stan laughed. 'The farmer probably wouldn't agree with you – they're eating his crops.'

'So where are we going then, Stan?'

He looked blank. 'I suppose we'll go wherever the wind takes us. It's a bit like life, really! We have our own plans and ideas, but none of us really knows what will happen next.'

Florence took hold of Stan's hand. 'That's true. After all, this time last year I would never have thought that I would be flying in a hot-air balloon with a kind, gentle, charming gentleman.'

Suddenly the conversation was interrupted by a commotion among their fellow travellers.

'What is it?' Florence asked.

She and Stan listened carefully as the pilot raised his voice to speak to the passengers. 'The cloud and weather conditions are just right for us to go up above the clouds today – if you would like to.'

There were various nods of agreement and excited murmurs. The pilot took that as being a yes. The burners roared into action, and the balloon began to rise in the sky.

Florence held tightly on to Stan's hand as the balloon entered into the cloud.

'It's like being in a really thick fog,' she commented as she pulled her collar up around her neck with the other hand. 'It's quite chilly.'

For what seemed like ages, the balloon rose up through the cloud, until suddenly it burst through into blazing sunshine and bright blue sky. Moments later, the pilot turned off the burner.

'This is perfect!' Florence said, overwhelmed. 'It's so silent and beautiful.' She pointed. 'Look at the silhouette of the balloon on top of the cloud.'

'It's like entering into another world completely,' Stan commented, in total amazement.

'It's like a dream,' Florence added. 'Not just the balloon trip and the beautiful outlook, but being here and sharing it with you, Stan.'

'That's a sweet thing to say. And I feel like that about being here with you.'

'The thing with dreams, though, is that we have to wake up from them.'

Stan smiled. 'Sometimes we can live out our dreams. Where would we be without hopes and dreams to follow? And they're worth fighting for – that's why you shouldn't give up on the future of Henry's Stud and Equestrian Centre.'

Florence nodded. 'You're right.'

At that moment the burner roared into action once again. But the time passed all too quickly.

Stan and Florence looked over the side of the basket and saw the 4x4 and trailer waiting outside a nearby field for their return. Following instructions from the pilot, they prepared themselves for what could be a bumpy landing. As they approached the ground, the passengers realised that their landing site was to be a meadow that had obviously recently contained a large herd of cattle.

'We're going to have to mind where we tread when we land!' Florence exclaimed.

Suddenly there was a loud bang as the point of impact came. Moments later, the envelope of the balloon lay limp in the field. The recovery team hurried across and began to dismantle everything, ready to pack away in the trailer.

'We'll have a glass of champagne or orange juice in a moment, before we go back,' the pilot promised.

Florence squeezed Stan's hand. 'That sounds nice!'

Twenty

Isabel was waiting for the two travellers when the recovery vehicles dropped them off at the launch site.

'How was it?' she asked excitedly.

Aunty Florence gave Isabel a big hug. 'It was absolutely amazing.'

Isabel looked questioningly at Stan.

'It really was!' he said.

After describing how it felt to go above the cloud, the topic turned towards hopes and dreams.

'You must never give up, Isabel,' Stan urged. 'I was saying that to Florence in the balloon.'

'He's right,' Aunty Florence confirmed. 'Mustn't give in to the bullies and let them crush our spirits.'

Isabel nodded in agreement. But inwardly she felt nervous about the future, and frightened of the bullies. 'OK.'

When they arrived home, Karen was finishing off tidying up the yard. As Isabel got out of the car, she breathed in the sweet smell of hay. The yard was quiet, except for the contented sound of horses pulling at their hay nets. Basil sat at his dish, crunching cat biscuits, and Colin was contentedly sniffing near one of the gateposts.

'How was it?'

'Absolutely amazing. You should go up in a balloon!' Stan replied.

Aunty Florence cracked a rare grin. 'Wonderful! It's been one of my ambitions for years. That, and owning a red 1950s-style motorcycle.'

Isabel stared at her. 'Oh!'

'I'd better go in and do some dinner,' Aunty Florence continued. 'Stan will be staying – hope that's all right?'

'Of course Stan can stay,' Karen replied with a twinkle in her eye. 'After all, he's almost one of the family now.'

Isabel frowned at her friend, shaking her head, but to little avail.

Karen walked across the yard towards the office humming a 'Wedding March' and shaking her bunch of keys in accompaniment.

It was an excited Isabel who scurried into the kitchen a few days later, holding up the local paper.

'"*Local Equestrian Centre and Stud Farm Faces Closure*",' she read out at the top of her voice. 'There's a wonderful photograph of Diana, as well.'

Karen looked up sharply from her toast and marmalade.

Isabel sensed that she had said the wrong thing, and tried to rectify it. 'It's very complimentary of Henry too.'

Aunty Florence peered over Isabel's shoulder, in an attempt to read what the paper said. 'Does it talk about that ruthless bully, Crawford-Smith?'

Isabel shook her head. 'They have to be very careful what they publish. They don't want to be sued.'

'Or to get on the wrong side of Crawford-Smith,' Karen added.

Ben wandered into the kitchen, still in his dressing gown. 'Do I smell fresh coffee?'

Isabel filled up a mug with coffee, put in a teaspoon of sugar and began stirring it vigorously, so that the liquid slopped over the side. 'Here you are.'

Karen's husband flopped down into a chair and began to sip his morning fix of caffeine. 'Anything good in the paper?'

Isabel held the open newspaper right in front of Ben. 'Look: it's the article about the centre. It's a good write-up.'

'Well, I hope it brings some money in.'

'It's not just about money,' Isabel replied indignantly. 'It's about achieving our aims, fulfilling hopes and dreams – and not allowing the bullies to win.'

Ben drained his mug of coffee. 'Any more where that came from?'

'You shouldn't drink so much coffee; it's not good for you,' Karen commented.

Ben ignored her as he reached for the pot.

Aunty Florence took the newspaper from Isabel and began to read what it said, eventually commenting, 'It is a good article, and she has given contact details. Now I suppose we just wait.'

Karen jumped to her feet. 'And while we're waiting, we need to get washed and dressed and out to work.'

Ben smiled. 'I'm working from home today.'

'Well, you can still get washed and dressed and get to work.'

Ben laughed and Karen gave him a kiss on the cheek. Isabel was so relieved that everything was OK with him, and that the old diary wasn't Ben's, and that there wasn't a big problem to deal with there, that she didn't hear the house phone ring at first. Then she did, and answered it.

It was Archie.

'I've just been reading the article. It's a good bit of publicity.'

Isabel thanked him profusely for his support. But Archie seemed reluctant to put the phone down.

'Is everything OK?' Isabel asked, concerned.

He coughed loudly. 'I'm getting over a chest infection. When you're my age, it's always more difficult to make a recovery.'

'But you've been to the doctor, haven't you?'

Archie grunted. 'There's a limit to what they can do.'

'Well, you take care. Keep warm and if I can do anything to help…'

Archie thanked her and said a brief goodbye.

As Isabel busied herself around the yard that morning, she kept thinking about him – and shot up a quick prayer.

Stan arrived unexpectedly after lunch. He had arrived several times without notice now that he was driving again.

'You look nice, Florence,' he observed.

Isabel had noticed that Aunty Florence was dressing much less severely these days, and was even doing her hair differently. 'Lovely to see you, Stan. Have you seen the article in the paper?'

Stan removed his dark-blue blazer, which had obviously seen better days, and hung it on the back of one of the kitchen chairs. 'Yes, my dear Florence. It was a good article.'

'Shall I go and leave you two lovebirds alone?' Isabel asked, with a wicked smile.

'Of course not,' Aunty Florence replied, playfully. 'We've got nothing to talk about that's private.'

Stan sat down with a sigh.

'What is it, Stan?' Isabel remarked.

He cleared his throat. 'I had a telephone call from the council. They want Roy's flat cleared.'

'But that's not your responsibility. What about his son? Why can't he do that?' Isabel said.

'Apparently he's too busy – so he told the council. So they rang me. I've been dealing with Roy's correspondence with the council for some time. In fact, it was me who told them that Roy had died. They said that Roy's son doesn't want any furniture or ornaments kept – any personal photographs or papers are to be put into a safe deposit box in town to await his collection when he's in the area.'

'What a cheek!' Aunty Florence exclaimed. 'After all you've done for Roy in the past, and now his son expects you to clear the flat.'

'He has organised and paid for the safe deposit box.'

Isabel left the kitchen briefly and returned with her laptop. 'I just thought I'd have a look to see if there have been any emails from the article.'

Isabel opened up her laptop, and the matter of the house clearance was left for the moment.

'So are there any emails in response to the article?' Stan asked.

Isabel scrolled through the list.

'Enjoyed reading the article and hope everything works out OK,' Isabel read.

'No offer of funding?' Stan enquired.

Isabel shook her head.

'Just won the lottery. How much would you like? Ha! Ha!' Isabel looked at Stan. 'Some people are just sick!'

'Don't take it to heart, love,' Aunty Florence said, in a consoling voice. 'Some people have a very strange sense of humour.'

Isabel sighed. 'Nothing useful.'

'So what do we do now?' Aunty Florence asked.

'Well,' Isabel began, 'I'm going to get my mare across to Thunder Bay as soon as she's ready, and have her put into foal. And then we're all going to get on with running this place. And then we're going to keep looking for a way to keep it open.'

'And I'm going to clear Roy's flat out, and help you all in any way I can,' Stan said, decisively.

Aunty Florence gave him an affectionate pat on the hand. 'You're such a good man, Stan.'

'Karen and Ben need to get that letter written to try to get sponsorship for Henry as soon as possible,' Isabel said firmly.

She heard a reply. Ben was leaning against the doorpost, smiling. 'OK, we'll get it done. I can take a hint!'

Twenty-one

'Who were you phoning?' Karen asked as she came into the kitchen for morning coffee.

Isabel was almost beside herself with excitement as she placed her phone into her pocket. 'Diana is ready to go to Thunder Bay. So I was phoning Matthew to see if it's OK to take her over.'

'I see!'

'Is it alright if I use the horse lorry, please?'

'Yes, of course. You don't need to ask.'

'I do,' Isabel replied, 'because I need you to drive it! Please.'

'OK. I don't have any lessons to take until later this afternoon.'

Isabel clasped her mug of coffee in her hands and suddenly looked at the window. 'Raining!'

Colin looked up from his bed and barked loudly.

Karen smiled. 'He likes the rain.'

'He's excited about the future! What about you? Are you a little bit excited that a new chapter could be beginning for the centre?'

'I'll tell you what would excite me: someone phoning up to say that they're prepared to put up the money to buy this place for us. The news that Crawford-Smith is going to emigrate to Australia would excite me.' Karen shook her head. 'Listen to me moaning away. I'll try to be excited for you, Isabel.' She walked over to the cupboard. 'Let's have some chocolate. Life always looks better after having chocolate!'

After a chocolate bar each, Isabel and Karen went out into the yard. Everywhere smelled fresh after the shower of rain. It was brightening up, the clouds were dispersing and the sun was breaking through.

Isabel produced a tatty-looking packet of mints from her pocket. 'Want one?'

Karen carefully placed a mint into her mouth and began to suck noisily, almost choking with the strength of the flavour.

'We might need these to persuade your horse to get into the lorry.'

'You get the lorry over and I'll put a headcollar onto Diana.'

Isabel glanced at the old lorry as Karen disappeared into the office to collect the keys. To say that the vehicle had seen better days was an understatement. The varnish had long since flaked off the wooden body and rust had attacked the dark-blue paintwork of the cab. A cloud of smoke enveloped the stable yard as the old lorry roared into action. Isabel began to cough as she walked her horse across.

As Karen got out of the cab, after moving the lorry into the middle of the yard, Isabel shouted over to her. 'We could do with a new horse lorry from those sponsors of yours.'

Karen lowered the ramp carefully. 'They'll probably just offer me a bridle.'

'You never know.'

Alec stood close by with some horse and pony nuts in his cloth cap – just in case.

'It's a little while since she's travelled anywhere,' Isabel said in anticipation, before even reaching the ramp.

Alec grinned. 'Don't talk it up; she might be fine.'

As Isabel approached the horse lorry, she could sense the mare's slight anxiety. 'It's OK, girl. Come on.'

Diana looked down at the ramp, snorted loudly and pulled back.

'Steady!'

Anxious not to upset the mare too much, Isabel quietly approached the lorry once again, talking to her all the time. Suddenly Henry neighed loudly. Diana raised her head and pricked her ears.

'Come on. You've been on the lorry before,' Isabel urged.

Even the temptation of food didn't work.

Moments later, with his cap back on his head, Alec walked across with Max. 'What about putting Max into the lorry first? Let them travel together for company.'

'Good idea,' Karen replied.

Max was a 'pro' – he walked straight up the ramp.

'Come on, girl,' Isabel confidently led the way and Diana followed without a second thought.

The journey was uneventful – although Karen moaned about driving the lorry along the narrow, twisty Norfolk country roads.

It seemed strange to leave Diana behind, but Isabel knew she would be in good hands. It was exciting to see the plan beginning to unfold. It felt like a step of faith. And that felt right.

At dinner that night, there was some argument about what Ben and Karen should ask for in their letter to the potential sponsors.

'I can't believe you haven't done this yet!' Isabel exclaimed, exasperated.

'We can't agree on the wording,' Ben told her.

'Well, I don't think we should be too greedy,' Isabel said.

Karen shook her head. 'Says she who suggested we might get a new horse lorry out of this.'

'I was only joking.'

Aunty Florence sighed. 'I think we need to ask for enough; otherwise, if we don't ask, we won't get. After all, sponsors do sometimes provide very smart lorries with living accommodation and everything.'

'It might be best not to go into too much detail at this stage.' Ben squeezed a large dollop of tomato sauce onto the side of his plate. 'Maybe we should just tell them about the centre, Henry, the breeding programme for quality coloured horses, and see if they would be interested in talking about a sponsorship deal.'

'If only Stan were here,' Aunty Florence pondered. 'He's so wise.'

It was eventually decided that it would be mainly an informative letter, although mention would be made of the need for finances, a new horse lorry and other equipment.

Ben drafted a letter, they all agreed it, and he pressed 'send'.

It was an elated Stan who arrived at the equestrian centre a few days later.

'Whatever is it?' Aunty Florence asked as she gave him a hug. 'You've been using aftershave – must be a special occasion.'

'What's happened, Stan? Have you won the lottery?' Karen asked, glancing up from her breakfast.

'Who's won the lottery?' Ben enquired, as he wandered into the kitchen, clutching his phone.

Even Colin barked and wagged his tail.

'Well, not quite the lottery.' Stan grinned as he reached into his inside pocket and produced a brown envelope. He pulled out a sheet of official-looking notepaper. 'A bit of a surprise when I received this yesterday. I didn't even know he had any money to speak of.'

'Stan, what are you talking about?' Aunty Florence demanded. 'You're not making any sense.'

'The letter is from Roy's solicitor, concerning the will. I didn't realise he had anything of any value.' Stan paused. 'Well he didn't really have any *thing* of any value.'

'Do get to the point!' Aunty Florence cried.

Stan began again. 'Well, it would appear that Roy had been putting aside a little money every so often into a bank account, for a rainy day. He had accumulated several hundred pounds. And he's left it to me. So I'd like you all to have it towards buying the centre.'

Isabel got up and put the kettle onto the range. 'No, Stan. Roy gave the money to you, to say thank you for all your kindness to him.'

'She's right,' Karen agreed. 'You should use the money to buy something for yourself.'

Aunty Florence nodded her head. 'Yes, Stan.'

'Absolutely.' Ben turned to go back to his work.

Stan looked deep in thought. 'What about if I were to buy a nice coloured mare that we could cover with Henry – that could be part of the breeding programme?'

Karen looked pensive. 'We still don't have a permanent home for this breeding programme. We don't want to have too many horses to home if things go wrong.'

Isabel was exasperated. 'Karen! Where is your faith? You have to believe that things will work out somehow!' She turned to Stan. 'I think it's a wonderful idea. We should start looking as soon as possible.'

In the evening, Ben, Karen, Isabel, Aunty Florence and Stan were sitting in the lounge listening to music. The atmosphere was calm and relaxed. Isabel was curled up on a large, comfy sofa, half asleep beside the log fire.

'It was nice of Roy to remember you in his will, wasn't it?' Aunty Florence commented.

'I suppose.'

Isabel put her head on one side, questioningly.

Stan smiled. 'I'm sorry. I wasn't being ungrateful. Yes, of course it was good of Roy to leave his savings to me. I just…' He paused. 'It would have been nice if Roy's son had sent a letter or a card, acknowledging… Well, I suppose I shouldn't expect thanks or even acknowledgement for helping Roy. I did it because he was a friend, a neighbour, a good man.'

'But what did his son do that made him so distant from his father and never able to have time to have a chat with you?' Aunty Florence asked.

Stan yawned. 'Just business. Whatever it is he does, it takes him abroad quite a lot. The few occasions when he found time to see his dad, it was a very fleeting visit. I never bumped into him while I was in and out of Roy's.' The old clock on the mantelpiece suddenly chimed. 'Nine o'clock. I ought to be going.'

Aunty Florence leaned forward and gave her friend a peck on the cheek. 'You did your best to help Roy, never expecting anything in return – not even a kind word from his son.'

'Ah, well.' Stan looked a little embarrassed. 'Must go! See you soon.'

Isabel got up. 'I think I'm going up to my room now; there's more praying to be done.'

'It's worth a try!' Karen commented. She raised her eyebrows. 'Yes, I did say that!'

Isabel smiled at her, and Aunty Florence squeezed her hand. 'You keep praying, dear. Just keep praying.'

Twenty-two

May

Ben, Karen, Isabel, Aunty Florence and Alec sat at the big table in the dining room, enjoying dinner. Colin was lying stretched out under Isabel's chair, and even Basil the cat had sneaked onto the hearth rug, trying not to be noticed. The room was filled with the aroma of lamb and mint sauce and horsy jodhpurs. There was an atmosphere of despondency.

'I don't think plan B is going to work,' Isabel said, reluctantly, as she endeavoured to fill her upturned fork with peas.

'Well, we've had no offers of financial help from all the publicity we've received,' Ben agreed.

Karen helped herself to some more mint sauce. 'So what do you suggest?'

With a mouth full of peas, Isabel tried to explain her thoughts. 'Well, you know Ben told us about the neighbours being pressurised to sell up their properties to Crawford-Smith...'

'I'm not sure I said *pressurised*,' Ben corrected her.

'OK. But they are, though, aren't they?' Isabel began to move the salt and pepper mills, mint sauce and jug of gravy around to a strategic area of the table. 'Call it plan C. Imagine the pepper mill is us, the salt mill is George from next door, the mint sauce is Doreen's fresh crab and samphire stall, the bread rolls are David and Caroline's bungalow, and the jug of gravy is Graham and Patricia's pig farm. Oh, and the sugar bowl is Sid and Kath's. Crawford-Smith's plans won't work if the others don't agree to sell to him.'

'So what do we do?' Ben asked.

Aunty Florence interjected. 'I know what you're saying. We need to invite them round to dinner or something, and see if we can get them to agree not to sell.'

Isabel grinned. 'That's right!'

Karen looked sceptical and Ben appeared worried. 'Just because the others won't sell, it doesn't mean Crawford-Smith won't still buy this place and develop it in some other way,' he pointed out.

Alec glanced up from his plate. 'No, but he might be less enthusiastic to buy.'

'And at least Crawford-Smith wouldn't be having things all his own way,' Isabel said.

The next day, Isabel and Aunty Florence set out in the early morning sunshine delivering dinner invitations to the neighbours.

'Do you suppose they'll come?'

'Most people will go out for a free meal,' Isabel said, a little cynically – until she thought better of it. 'Sorry, that sounded awful, didn't it?'

'I know what you mean, though,' Aunty Florence replied. 'Well, let's hope they do come.'

As they walked further up the road, they were met by a strong aroma of pigs.

'You'd think we'd get used to the smell from the pig farm, wouldn't you?' Isabel commented. 'But I certainly don't. And what's more, if Graham and Patricia decide to come to dinner, I wonder if they'll bring the smell with them!'

Isabel hurried into the yard, holding her breath, ready to slip the invitation through their letter box.

'Hello, Isabel.' She looked round to see Patricia leaning over one of the pigsty doors. 'Fancy seeing you here.'

Isabel felt that it would be very impolite not to stop and chat for a moment. 'We're having a dinner party for all the neighbours in a couple of days.'

Patricia smiled. 'That'll be nice. Graham and I don't get asked out much – I don't know why.'

'Fancy that!' Isabel sneezed loudly, as the aroma of pigs seemed to catch her in the back of her nose. 'Excuse me!'

'You can put us down to come then, please, love.'

A few days later, Karen and Isabel were trying to work out how to seat fourteen people at the farmhouse dining room. Fortunately, there was a gate-legged table on the landing, which they were able to bring down and set up in addition to the big dining table – together with chairs from the kitchen and the bedrooms. In the meantime, Aunty Florence was peeling the mass of vegetables in the kitchen.

Ben and Alec had agreed to lend a hand with the dinner; they would organise the washing-up afterwards. In the meantime, they seemed to be taking on the role of observers.

'Have you decided what you're going to say about Crawford-Smith this evening, Ben?' Karen asked.

'We need to be a little bit tactful in how we address the situation,' Isabel emphasised. 'After all, they might be madly in favour of selling up their properties for whatever reason.'

'I agree,' Aunty Florence said, wiping her face with the back of her hand.

'Is Stan coming?' asked Isabel.

Aunty Florence smiled contentedly. 'He's coming – all being well.'

As Karen and Isabel set the tables, the aroma of roast beef began to fill the old farmhouse. Colin walked around the kitchen with his nose in the air.

'There's nothing for you!' Aunty Florence reprimanded. 'Not yet, anyway!'

As evening approached, the guests began to arrive. In their enthusiasm, Graham and Patricia were the first, and Isabel was relieved that there was not even a faint aroma of pigs. The next to arrive were Sid and Kath, from the house beyond the pig farm. Approaching their seventies, they had chosen to retire in north Norfolk following many delightful holidays in the area. Close behind them were David and Caroline from the big bungalow, set right back from the road – almost out of sight to passers-by. They both commuted into Norwich each day, to work. The last two to arrive were George from next door, and Doreen from the old flint cottage with the crab and samphire stall by the roadside.

During the main course, Ben led into discussion about Crawford-Smith. 'I understand that we could all be moving on soon, if Mr Crawford-Smith has his way.'

A long silence followed. Isabel felt that maybe Ben had touched a raw nerve – either that, or maybe their guests were not willing to discuss their private lives in front of so many people.

'Not that he's received planning permission for his scheme – yet!' Karen added.

Another long silence followed, only broken by George asking for the horseradish sauce.

Eventually Graham spoke up. 'Crawford-Smith has made us a very good offer. It's very tempting, especially bearing in mind the price of pork at the moment.'

Caroline carefully emptied her mouth before speaking. 'David and I would find it much more convenient to be living closer to Norwich, especially in the winter months.'

Sid chuckled nervously, causing his stomach to wobble precariously. 'There's a lot to be said for sheltered housing at our age.'

Kath nodded in agreement.

Doreen opened her mouth as if to say something, but nothing came out. Then she rubbed her chin knowingly and opened her mouth again. 'Suppose it was a bit quiet last year…'

George obviously felt that he was expected to make some kind of comment. 'Well, all I can say is that I'm quite happy living where I am. I don't want to move, and I resent the pressure that this Crawford-Smith fellow is applying to try to get me to sell up to him.'

Following George's comments, there was silence. Then Doreen spoke up again.

'To be honest, I don't really want to go.'

This seemed to open the way for the others to express how they really felt, deep down. It soon became apparent that in fact no one really wanted to move, but they felt intimidated by Crawford-Smith.

'We're in a rather different position from all of you,' Ben explained. 'We don't own this property, and it's going to auction soon. So unless we can raise the money to buy it – which seems highly unlikely – it probably won't make too much difference to us if Crawford-Smith's project falls through or not. We're still likely to be made homeless.'

Isabel interrupted. 'But at least by working together we can prevent Crawford-Smith from bullying you all just so he gets his own way. We need to work together to stand up to the bullies in society.'

George nodded. 'You're absolutely right. Why should these rich and powerful people always get their own way – especially if it's through unethical, bullying tactics?'

The others voiced their support to opposing Crawford-Smith and the development plan, both by not selling their properties and by aiming to oppose the plans he had sent in to the planning authorities.

But as they left, Isabel wondered how brave they'd all be in the morning, or if Crawford-Smith were to pile on more pressure.

Ten days later, Ben was in deep conversation on the phone, while Isabel and Karen were listening in.

'Well, that's good news!' Ben exclaimed, as he put the receiver back into the charger. 'The planners said that the plans for Crawford-Smith's development are in the fairly early stages yet. No permission has been granted. We still have every opportunity to fight against it, although the redevelopment might be looked upon in quite a favourable light, bearing in mind the potential new job opportunities and so on.' He paused thoughtfully. 'Probably the most powerful tool against the redevelopment is our neighbours refusing to sell their properties. Unfortunately, we don't have that same opportunity to fight.'

Isabel and Karen nodded.

'We need to keep the momentum going, though,' Isabel said. 'We need to keep supporting each other, helping the neighbours to resist the whole development.'

Aunty Florence took a large, brightly coloured tin out of the cupboard. 'Anyone for one of Karen's Norfolk shortcakes?'

Isabel took one. 'Crawford-Smith is such a nasty bully, isn't he?'

'The trouble is that so often people like that get away with it!' Karen pointed out. 'Big, unscrupulous companies!'

'That's why we mustn't just roll over,' Isabel said, quietly.

Ben agreed to contact the neighbours again, to encourage them to write petitions and to send letters of complaint to the local council, and to the press.

Several days later, Isabel was leaning over the stable half-door, sharing her feelings with her four-legged friend and confidante. Diana had only just arrived back from the stallion.

'Not long to go now,' she said, with sadness in her voice. 'The auction is still going ahead, and we still don't have the money to buy Henry's Stud and Equestrian Centre.'

Diana neighed loudly, as if in agreement.

'Even if the neighbours don't agree to sell to Crawford-Smith, we're not safe.' She took a deep breath. 'That's not to say that he won't send his heavies around to change their minds.'

Diana walked over to the door and nuzzled up to her owner.

Isabel frowned. 'Even if the planners turn the scheme down, knowing Crawford-Smith, he could still buy this property just to spite us.'

'Talking to your horse again?' Karen stood behind her friend. 'Do you think she understands?'

Isabel rubbed Diana's neck affectionately. 'I'm just having a bit of a negative moment, and she's a good listener. Sorry!'

Karen put a hand on her shoulder. 'You're allowed to have a negative moment, but we mustn't give up. We can't let them win. You... you just keep praying.' Isabel looked at her, and Karen smiled. 'Ben has contacted all the neighbours again, and they're still agreeing to oppose Crawford-Smith. We'll just have to wait and see what happens.'

Twenty-three

Everyone was sitting around the breakfast table, chatting excitedly about the day ahead.

Suddenly there was a loud clunk as some mail dropped through the letter box. Colin hurried through into the hall, barking excitedly.

'I'll go. Who knows, it might be a windfall. We could do with some money – £500,000 would be nice,' Karen said, ironically, as she got up from her chair. 'Or even a little bit more than that.'

'We could certainly do with some good news,' Ben remarked. 'Let's face it, it's not really likely to be anything more than junk mail or bills.' He buttered another piece of toast.

'OK, I won't get it. I won't bother,' Karen snapped, sitting down again.

Isabel sighed, stood up and went to get the post.

Moments later she hurried back, beaming, holding a letter up in the air. 'It looks important.'

It was a large envelope with gold lettering and a brightly coloured horse's head on the front.

'Maybe it's a potential sponsor,' Karen said in eager anticipation, grabbing the envelope from Isabel and ripping it open.

'What does it say?'

'Shhh!' Karen was intently reading the enclosed letter. 'Right: "We would like you to come and meet with us to discuss the possibility of our company offering sponsorship for your Hanoverian stallion, Henry." Who fancies a day in the outskirts of London, next week?'

Hands went up. At the very least, this would provide a day of relief from the ever-present stress of the situation at the centre.

Everyone, except Aunty Florence who still used a paper diary, got their phones out to put the date in. Isabel was instantly reminded of the old diary she had discovered in the yard. 'I need to speak to Aunty Florence,' she mumbled under her breath, 'soon!'

Karen looked at her friend inquisitively. 'Did you say something?'

Isabel shook her head. 'Nothing important!'

The following Wednesday, Karen, Isabel and Aunty Florence made an early start. The address of the potential sponsor had been placed into the satnav on Karen's phone, so they were ready to go. It wasn't long before Aunty Florence got bored and started munching crisps as she sat on the back seat.

Isabel giggled. 'You've only just eaten breakfast.'

'Can you not make so much noise, with your crunching?' Karen glanced in the rear-view mirror, obviously irritated.

'Would you like one?' Aunty Florence teased.

'They're fattening,' said Karen. 'You don't want to eat too many of them – you'll never fit into your wedding dress.'

'Cheeky!' responded Aunty Florence.

Isabel changed the subject. 'Do you think this company will supply us with a new horse lorry?'

'I hope so,' Karen replied.

'I'm just hoping for a good day out,' Aunty Florence quipped.

'You really are in a good mood these days!' Karen observed, and she smiled.

Isabel and Karen had done their research into the company: it boasted of providing everything for the horse owner, all under one roof.

'We could end up with a new horse lorry, saddles, bridles, rugs and even a set of show jumps,' Isabel suggested, brushing her hair back.

'You're ever hopeful, Isabel. Let's just wait and see what they offer us, shall we?'

There were a lot of hold-ups on the journey: the traffic was really heavy and there were numerous sets of traffic lights for roadworks.

Eventually, the directions on the phone indicated that the destination was half a mile away.

The company's headquarters were certainly very impressive. As they drove into the car park they noticed a brand-new horse lorry with a large 'For Sale' notice on the windscreen.

Karen stared at it. 'That one would do us nicely!'

'Oh dear! I am really stiff after the journey,' Aunty Florence grumbled as she struggled out of the car.

Isabel hurried round to give her a helping hand. 'Where do we go in?'

Karen led the way. 'It looks like the reception over there.' She pointed.

The reception area was very tastefully decorated, with a large mural of a rose-grey horse going around a set of brightly coloured show jumps. A young girl sat at a large reception desk, surrounded by a selection of equine products. She peered between a dressage saddle, a double bridle and a stack of veterinary products for horses.

'Good morning. Can I help you?'

Karen introduced herself. 'We have an appointment at 11.30.'

'Good morning, my name is Shaun Williams.' A tall, slightly overweight man came over to them. He had a round face and was accompanied by a slim woman, who had an air of sophistication.

'I'm Monica Wright.' She introduced herself and her colleague as being part of the management team. 'We will be your hosts today.'

Monica handed their guests a timetable of the proceedings. They were to begin with a meeting in the office at 11.30, with lunch at 12.30 and a tour around the headquarters and factory at 2.00, finishing with tea and biscuits in the reception area.

'Will you be able to give us a decision today?' Karen enquired.

After a moment of silence, Monica shook her head.

Shaun laughed reassuringly. 'Obviously we will need to take your application for sponsorship to the board before we can give a decision. But we will endeavour to let you know as soon as possible.'

'Let's go into the office,' Monica invited. 'We need to find out a bit more about Henry, and the centre, and no doubt there will be questions you will want to ask us.'

It was Shaun's cheery disposition that kept an air of informality about the meeting, while Monica asked some very probing questions. Obviously, the company needed to be assured that it would receive a significant benefit from its investment, particularly if it was to be a considerable one.

Then Monica challenged Karen with the one question Isabel had been dreading. Whatever would her friend say in reply?

'So what would it look like for you to receive sponsorship from us?'

'Sorry?' Karen looked confused. 'I don't understand.'

'What kind of settlement were you looking for? Financial? Equipment? Saddlery? Or maybe a combination of everything?' Shaun asked.

Karen explained the whole situation with regard to the possibility of losing the centre. 'So, though we would like a new horse lorry, saddlery and show jumps, ultimately we would appreciate a financial settlement towards the purchase of the centre.'

At this, Shaun looked shocked and Monica gasped.

'Let me stop you there,' Shaun began diplomatically. 'We would not be considering anything of that magnitude. Our usual settlements involve probably a new saddle, a show jump with our company name on it, and maybe a small financial settlement to cover some of the competition entry fees.'

Isabel smiled. 'OK! That would be good, thanks.'

The rest of the visit was an anticlimax, so what was supposed to be a day of excitement and being encouraged turned out to be a bit of a disappointment. As Isabel drove home, little was said. All that could be heard was the sound of traffic and the satnav on Karen's phone.

When they arrived home, Isabel decided it was time to confront Aunty Florence about the diary she had found. She went to her sock drawer – and then she saw the date on the front. The diary wasn't just old, it was *very* old: five years old! Why hadn't she seen that before?

Coming out of her room, she found Aunty Florence coming up the staircase.

'I think this is yours.' Isabel held the diary up. 'I found it in the yard.'

'My diary! I wondered where I'd dropped it. Good of you to return it.' Aunty Florence snatched the little book. 'I hope you didn't read it.'

Isabel was about to give her apologies and make some appropriate excuse for looking at some of the contents, but instead she found herself blurting out, 'Why a red motorcycle?'

'You *did* read it! It's private!' Then she muttered, 'A 500 single – just me and the elements!' Then she hurried off to her room.

In the evening, Aunty Florence was standing in the dining room on her own when Isabel walked in on her. She was just in time to hear her say in a soft voice, '*We regret to inform you…*'

Aunty Florence jumped. 'Oh, it's you, Isabel. I didn't expect you. It was just something I remembered from the diary. Some bad news, but it doesn't matter now. It's in the past.'

158

'It's OK. You don't need to explain yourself. But I think I do. I'm sorry.'

Aunty Florence didn't seem to hear her.

'I'm such a silly old woman. People say don't put all your eggs in one basket, and now…'

Suddenly the door banged. Colin began to bark excitedly. The others had arrived home.

'I need to tell you something. I need to tell all of you!' Aunty Florence said, decisively.

'But the diary – I'm sorry…'

But Aunty Florence had swept out of the room.

Later that evening, everyone – except for Aunty Florence – was sitting in the lounge watching the large-screen TV, eating crisps and chocolate. The lights were dimmed and Colin was lying stretched out on the brown hearthrug, fast asleep.

Suddenly, Aunty Florence walked in.

'I have something important to tell you,' she announced.

Karen looked up. 'What's that, then, Aunty?'

Isabel feared that she might reveal things that should remain private. 'You don't have to say anything.'

'About what?' Ben enquired, still staring at the TV screen.

Aunty Florence smiled. 'I *do* have to say something. I should have spoken about my situation years ago, instead of allowing it to fill me with bitterness. But I was so ashamed.'

Ben suddenly turned from the television to look at Aunty Florence. 'Does what you are going to say involve me?' He paused. 'It's getting late. Maybe now isn't the time.'

Aunty Florence ignored the remark. 'Switch that television off!'

Ben did so immediately, and the others stared at her.

'Five years ago,' she began, 'I asked Ben for some financial advice. I had some savings, including one or two substantial legacies, which I wanted to invest wisely to see me through my old age – together with my pension. There was a company that looked as if it was going to make a fortune, although it had no proven track record. Ben advised me to only put in what I could afford to lose, but I put in everything – I even re-mortgaged my house.'

'What?' Ben said in surprise.

'Let me finish. I lost everything: my savings, the house and my nest egg to see me through my old age.'

'But...'

'My present flat is rented. I have nothing. I am not the rich old lady you thought I was.'

There was a silence, broken only by the sound of Colin snoring on the hearth rug.

'Now do you see why I couldn't lend or give you the money to buy this place?'

Isabel turned to Ben. 'You told me that this business with Aunty Florence was about some silly incident at a wedding.'

'I lied. I'm so sorry. I was too embarrassed to tell you I'd given bad financial advice – although I did say not to invest everything in the one company. I knew she would have lost tens of thousands of pounds, but I never knew she'd lost everything.'

Isabel turned to Aunty Florence. 'Was that what the diary was all about? And did you...'

'Yes, dear, it was what the diary was all about. But no, I didn't run after all. I decided to stay and sort things out.'

'Diary? What diary?' Ben asked, bewildered.

'Ben,' Karen said firmly, 'I think you and I need to talk.'

Twenty-four

June

Isabel, Karen and Aunty Florence were sitting out in the sun, in the back garden of the old farmhouse, drinking homemade lemonade.

'Well done, Aunty Florence, this is lovely!' Isabel gulped down her last mouthful. 'Thanks for making it.'

Alec was chasing a wasp around the big apple tree in the middle of the lawn. 'Yes, thanks Aunty F.'

'The flower borders all need weeding,' Karen said, idly. 'That's the trouble with having a large garden.'

Isabel helped herself to some more lemonade. 'The vet should be coming this morning to do a manual examination of Diana, to see if she's in foal.'

'Stan will be pleased if she is.' Aunty Florence added, 'He should be coming over later today.'

Karen frowned. 'Does that mean I need to cook an extra portion of dinner tonight?'

'You don't mind him coming for dinner, do you?'

'She's just teasing you,' Isabel said, laughing loudly. 'Stop it, Karen.' She turned towards Aunty Florence. 'Of course she doesn't mind.'

Alec picked Colin up on his return to his chair and sat him on his lap. 'Which vet is coming today?'

'I believe Mr Monroe is coming, and he's bringing a Polish student vet with him.' Isabel looked in the brightly coloured biscuit tin, sitting on the table. 'Have we got any of those nice chocolate biscuits left?'

'Do you mean these?' Aunty Florence held up an empty packet. 'I'm afraid Stan and I finished them off last night before he went home.'

Colin suddenly jumped off Alec's lap, barking furiously.

'Must be the vet arriving,' Karen said.

Sure enough, the sound of a heavy 4x4 could be heard turning on to the gravel drive.

Mr Monroe reached into the boot of the 4x4, eventually pulling out his bag. He introduced his young colleague as Antoni. He laughed, 'And he speaks better English than I do.'

Antoni smiled as he put on a long plastic glove and began to cover it with lubricant. 'I think I am ready. Please could you show me where the mare is.'

It was a tense few minutes while the young vet examined Diana. He looked very serious.

'Anything?' Isabel asked, rubbing her hands together anxiously.

'Take your time, lad,' the older vet encouraged.

Suddenly Antoni grinned, and excitedly exclaimed, 'I can feel it. I can feel the signs of an embryo being present.'

Mr Monroe smiled at the anxious Isabel. 'Your mare is in foal, young lady – congratulations.'

Isabel squealed loudly, unable to contain herself. 'Diana is in foal!' She shouted across the yard, to anyone who might be listening.

Later that day, Stan arrived, carrying a bag of fruit scones.

Aunty Florence hurried out of the back door and embraced him affectionately. 'Isabel has something to tell you.'

Isabel rushed across the yard.

Stan looked questioningly at her. 'What is it?'

'This time next year, we'll have a wonderful little coloured colt foal.'

'You hope!' Aunty Florence added. 'It could be a bay filly.'

Stan clapped his hands together. 'We can hope that it will be a coloured colt, and of stallion quality. Any more news about the sponsorship?'

Isabel shook her head. 'Even if we do get it, it's not going to be enough to save us from Crawford-Smith.'

Stan looked disappointed. 'What about the neighbours? Has Ben heard anything back from them?'

Aunty Florence cleared her throat. 'Apparently, all the neighbours are still adamant about not selling their properties to Crawford-Smith but, despite them sending letters of objection and petitions, the planners still seem to be looking favourably on the development.'

Isabel could see that Stan was trying to think of something encouraging to say, to lift everyone's spirits. But the best he could come up with was, 'Let's all go inside and have a cup of tea and a scone to celebrate Diana being in foal.'

Stan had just finished buttering his scone when suddenly Aunty Florence turned to him. 'I have something to tell you.'

'Oh, really?'

'I don't have any money. I'm completely broke.'

He winked. 'That's all right, my dear; this is my treat.'

'No, no,' she argued. 'You don't understand. I mean that I don't have any money in savings accounts or other investments. My flat is not my own – in fact, I'm more or less broke!'

'Why are you telling me this?'

Isabel felt embarrassed for Aunty Florence. 'You don't need to keep telling everyone.'

'I'm no good to anyone.' Aunty Florence looked defeated. 'I can't help you and Karen to keep the stables, or even to keep a roof over our heads.'

Stan took her hand. 'Florence, I'm sure it's not your fault.'

'But we're still going to be homeless in August, whether it's my fault or not.'

'There has to be a way.' Isabel leaned back in her chair. 'If not, we'll find somewhere else. After all, Diana will be having a foal next spring.'

A couple of days later, Isabel asked Aunty Florence if she would like to accompany her and Colin on a walk through the woods.

'Summer is here at last!' Isabel exclaimed. 'Although there's a dark cloud in the distance.'

Aunty Florence looked up into the trees. 'These old oak and beech trees have seen a few summers in their time.'

The trees towered above the walkers, gently swaying in the breeze, leaves rustling as they did so. But it was a warm breeze. Red poppies danced about excitedly in the clearings, in rhythm with the trees. Isabel took a deep breath – it even smelled of summer.

Colin trotted happily off into the distance.

'Don't go too far,' Aunty Florence called after him. 'And don't go paddling in the stream!' But it was too late.

'It's OK,' Isabel reassured her. 'I put a towel in the car.'

As the two women walked along the twisty path, being careful to avoid the rabbit holes and tree stumps, there was a wonderful peacefulness.

'It's so quiet and beautiful here,' Isabel mused. 'I feel so relaxed and carefree. It seems hard to believe that our whole future could still be in jeopardy.'

'Mmm!' Aunty Florence replied.

'You feel it as well, don't you? I can tell.' Isabel persisted. 'Why aren't we frantically panicking?'

Aunty Florence smiled. 'Would it make any difference if we were?'

'No. I don't suppose it would.'

'Maybe our luck is in.'

Isabel stared at Aunty Florence. 'Do you really think our lives are controlled by nothing more than chance?'

Aunty Florence thought for a moment. 'It's what people say, isn't it?'

Isabel was about to respond when suddenly Colin came bounding up to her, jumped up and nearly knocked her over. 'Steady on, fella! Now look at me, I'm all wet from your paws.'

A short silence followed, as both women continued to enjoy the sights, sounds and smells of the woods.

Then Isabel grabbed Aunty Florence's hand playfully. 'But what about you and Stan? You do seem to be very fond of each other. Are there going to be wedding bells soon?'

'Oh, don't be silly. I'm too old to get married. Besides, I'm sure Stan could find someone more deserving of his wonderful kind and gentle personality than me.'

'If he loves you,' Isabel persisted, 'age doesn't come into it at all.'

Aunty Florence picked a dandelion that had gone to seed. 'I must admit, I am very fond of Stan. I don't think I've known anyone quite like him before: his temperament and honesty. I would be very tempted to say yes if he were to pop the question.'

Isabel leaned over and blew the seeds off the dandelion. 'Ohhh! So there *could* be wedding bells, then. I'll have to speak to Stan, tell him to get on with proposing to you.'

'Don't you dare do anything of the sort,' Aunty Florence laughed.

'I'm just kidding.'

'I know. A few months ago, who would have thought I would have been having this conversation with you.'

Isabel glanced at her phone. 'We probably ought to be getting back.' She held the palm of her hand up. 'It's beginning to rain.'

They sheltered under the trees for a while, and then turned towards the car park. It was only when they were back at the car that they noticed a rainbow in the distance.

'Promise,' Isabel mumbled to herself.

'What?'

'Promise!' Isabel repeated more decisively. 'In the Bible, God sends a rainbow as a sign that He will fulfil his promise to Noah, and future generations.'

'What's He promising you, then?'

Isabel thought deeply for a few minutes. 'I suppose I would like to think that He's going to make everything right with the centre.' She looked at the rainbow again. 'Do you know what rainbows remind me of?'

Aunty Florence shook her head.

'That God loves me. I suppose I want Him to care about what happens to me and love me unconditionally – like a good dad should.'

When they got home, it was sunny again. Aunty Florence disappeared indoors, and Karen wandered over from the tack room. She and Isabel stood in the sun, surveying the yard.

'This really is an amazing place, isn't it?' Karen said, a little sadly.

'Yes.'

'I'm going to really miss it. You know. If…'

'Wait! I know!' Isabel suddenly squealed. 'Why don't we organise a fun day for our clients, just to cheer us up?'

Karen put her hand above her eyes, to act as a shade from the sun, and gazed at the motley assortment of ponies that were happily grazing in the meadow next to the old flint barn.

'I'm sure the clients would enjoy that, and not just the younger ones,' she agreed. 'I expect the horses and ponies would enjoy it too.'

Isabel took out her phone and looked at the diary. 'So when are we going to hold this fun day?'

'Well, we can't do it this Saturday because we have rides booked in already, but we could do it next week.'

Isabel did a thumbs up. 'It won't need much organising. But it'll focus our minds on something, like a distraction.'

Karen laughed. 'Sounds good to me.'

Everyone had an early start on the morning of the fun day.

'I'll build the jumping course,' Isabel volunteered. 'And you can help me, Alec.'

Alec nodded. 'Where shall we start?'

'We want a course of eight small jumps in the outdoor school,' Karen said to them. 'And include a mixture of upright and spread fences.'

Isabel headed off towards the jump store, followed by Alec. 'We need twelve sets of jump wings, some planks, fillers and about twenty coloured poles.'

'I'll be in the pony meadow, setting up a dressage arena,' Karen shouted after them.

In the meantime, a number of the clients came in early to make sure all the horses and ponies were groomed and ready to tack up.

Later that morning, Karen, Isabel and Aunty Florence stood admiring the scene. All their own horses and ponies were tacked up ready, and the livery horses and ponies too. The row of black, wooden stables were all full, as were the adjoining pony stalls.

'The jumping course looks really impressive against the white background of the old farmhouse, doesn't it?' Aunty Florence commented. 'Such lovely colours. Someone ought to take some photos.'

'I already have!' Isabel said. 'I took some of the ponies' meadow, as well. I thought the big horse chestnut tree looked so amazing.'

Karen sighed. 'I don't want to lose all this. It would be awful if the bulldozers came in and this site was all redeveloped, wouldn't it?'

'Hello!'

Karen and Isabel turned round.

'Hannah!' Isabel exclaimed. She could hardly believe the sad girl she'd met in Diana's stable looked so happy and well. Helping at the stables on Saturdays was clearly agreeing with her.

She held out an envelope. 'Dad has given me the money to have a ride today. I'm booked in to go round the jumping course.'

'Great. You're getting really good, Hannah,' Isabel said, warmly.

'All because of you and Karen,' the girl replied, shyly.

Isabel smiled.

Alec seemed to spend much of his time being followed by small groups of girls who had come for the fun day — something he seemed to take in his stride. There was a large group of adults, on the bigger horses, waiting to go in to the dressage arena, whereas the younger riders, on the ponies, seemed to be queuing mainly for the jumping.

'Cyril will never manage to go round the jumping course clear,' Isabel heard one of the riders remark. Then she heard Hannah's quick reply.

'You'll be surprised what that pony can do!'

The girl who was riding Cyril sent the black and white cob away into a brisk trot around the arena, waiting for the bell to ring, indicating that they could start the course.

Ding, ding!

Cyril enthusiastically broke into a canter, as he approached the first jump — a small red upright. He cleared it with ease.

'Well done!' Isabel said under her breath.

By the time the combination reached the last jump — a fairly wide spread — Cyril had really got into the swing of things.

The rider gave him an extra strong squeeze with her legs, allowed with the reins, and the coloured cob flew over the fence, making a clear round.

'Well done!' Isabel praised the rider.

The next one into the jumping arena was Hannah. Alec led her in on Dotty.

Hannah seemed hesitant.

'You'll be OK on her, she loves jumping,' Alec told her.

'I know,' Hannah said, 'but the jumps look very big.'

'You can do it!' Isabel encouraged her.

A few minutes later Hannah was trotting round the arena on Dotty. Over the first jump with no problems. As she continued round the course, her confidence grew.

'Two more jumps, girl,' she said, excitedly – the planks and then the spread fence.

'Hooray!' Isabel shouted, as Hannah and Dotty came out of the arena.

Isabel presented them with a large blue rosette.

'Isabel, can I tell you something?' whispered Hannah. 'I really, really want to ride Cyril.'

'He's a bit big for you yet,' Isabel smiled. 'But maybe soon.'

As the light was beginning to fade, Karen came up to Isabel. 'It's been a wonderful day, hasn't it?'

Isabel nodded in agreement. 'How did the dressage go?'

'Really well. We've had a good turn out all round.'

'We just need to hope and pray that things work out in the future so that we can have many more such days,' Isabel responded.

Karen half-smiled. 'You need to keep praying.'

Alec came over, with Hannah alongside, excitedly chatting to him.

'Shall we start untacking the horses, now?' he asked.

Karen smiled. 'Sounds like a plan!'

Twenty-five

Stan seemed to be a little off his food, much to Florence's concern. They were out for dinner together at the local Indian restaurant. The manager had found them a nice quiet table for two in the corner.

'What is it, Stan? You've hardly touched your food this evening. You seem a little tense. I thought curry was one of your favourites. Was there something wrong with it? Wasn't it nice?'

Stan admitted that he loved the whole ambience of the Indian restaurant: the background music, the aroma of spices, and the care and attention given to them by the waiters and waitresses. 'There was nothing wrong with it, at all. It was up to their usual high standard. I just... I just...'

'You just what?'

'I've had something on my mind this evening – I'm sorry that it might have spoiled the evening to some extent.' He paused, taking a deep breath. 'I have something that I need to speak to you about, Florence.'

'Go on. What is it?'

At that moment the waiter approached the table. 'Would you like anything else, sir?'

'Oh, not now. Come back in a few minutes.' The waiter left, but Stan sighed. 'I was rude. Let me just go and apologise, before I say what I've got to say.'

He put his napkin down, left the table and returned a few minutes later.

'You're such a gentle and gracious person, Stan,' Florence commented. 'Now what do you want to talk to me about?'

Stan carefully lowered himself onto one knee, 'Florence, my dear…'

'What are you doing? Have you dropped your napkin? If you get down there, will you be able to get up again?' Florence asked. 'People are looking, Stan! Please get up and finish your food.'

'No, I haven't dropped my napkin! No, I probably won't be able to get up again! And let people look! Florence, I want the whole world to know how much I love you; and what's more, I want to spend the rest of my life with you.'

Aunty Florence interrupted. 'Please, Stan, do get up off the floor!' She leaned forward in a whisper. 'You know that I'm very fond of you, but now is not the time.'

'But…'

'Dear, sweet Stan, let's not rush into making such a significant decision. Can we at least wait until things have been sorted out with the centre?'

Stan tried to get to his feet. 'I think I'm going to need a hand, please, Florence.'

'Really!' Florence stood up, took hold of Stan's hands and helped him to his feet. 'Now do sit down, please.' She turned towards the other diners and said, in a loud voice, 'Show's over! Please get on with your meals.'

Stan signalled to the waiter. 'Could we have a refill of drinks, please?'

Moments later, drinks in front of them, Aunty Florence continued. 'I've been single all my life. I like my independence. I've only just found a family to be part of.' She heaved a sigh. 'But if I wanted to get married, it would be to you. Let's not rush into anything.'

Stan replied, 'You know I won't give up!'

'Well, I never said you couldn't ask me again,' Florence said, with a grin.

Twenty-six

The following day, Aunty Florence made an announcement in the kitchen. 'Please don't make any more quips about Stan and me being romantically involved. We have decided that we will not get be getting married for the foreseeable future, but will remain very close friends.'

'I won't be buying a new hat, then!' Isabel said, playfully.

'I will continue to be a regular visitor here, and I would still like to be involved with the new project to breed top-quality coloured horses!' Stan clarified.

'Of course!' they choroused.

'And I'm not going to give up asking Florence to be my wife,' Stan added, 'until she agrees.'

'Stan,' Isabel said, 'what's in that large, brown paper bag you're clutching so tightly? Could it possibly be a bag of jam doughnuts?'

He laughed. 'Well spotted. Come on, everyone, you must have one. We're celebrating today!'

'What are we celebrating, then?' Ben asked.

'We're celebrating that Florence has agreed to be my friend,' Stan confirmed. 'And that I won't give up.'

'Here's to determination!' Ben said.

Karen delicately nibbled at her doughnut, trying not to get it all over her fingers and face.

Isabel just took a large bite out of hers, face and hands covered in sugar, with jam dribbling down her chin. 'That's how to eat a jam doughnut,' she announced, triumphantly.

Aunty Florence preferred to have a plate and a small cake fork. 'Can I get you one as well, Stan?'

Ben took one into the other room with him, to eat while he worked.

Moments later, Isabel walked over to the kitchen sink to wash her hands and face. 'I enjoyed that, thanks, Stan.'

The phone started to ring. Karen hurried over to answer it. 'Hello, Henry's Stud Farm and Equestrian Centre...' She picked up a pencil, dragged the diary over and began to write some names down. 'And that's a class lesson for beginners – and you're all adults.'

As Karen put the phone down, Isabel looked across at the open page, and her heart sank. She read the names aloud: 'Madeleine Butler, Rosemary Penney and Heather Brown.'

'They're new customers, you won't know them,' Karen said excitedly. 'Good, isn't it? I'll put you down to take the lesson.'

Isabel swallowed hard. 'Yes, of course!'

Later that day, as Isabel busied herself around the yard, she couldn't get the three names out of her mind.

'I wonder if they've changed at all,' she mumbled to herself. 'A little older, maybe even a little wiser, but I wonder if they'll remember me.'

She also wondered if maybe she should speak with Aunty Florence – take her into her confidence. Isabel felt a shiver go down her back as she recalled the feelings of fear and vulnerability she had experienced as a young teenager – but she felt unable to share why.

That night, Isabel was restless, tossing and turning, unable to sleep or get comfortable. Thoughts raced relentlessly through her mind. What should she say? Could she forgive and forget?

Maybe she could forgive, but not forget – she could never forget. Was that true forgiveness?

She prayed:

Hi God. You know all about forgiveness – You are the God of forgiveness! I'm going to need some help tomorrow, please. I

need to do some big-time forgiving. Some spiritual amnesia is
required to be able to forgive and forget. Be with me as I face
one of my greatest fears over the next twenty-four hours.
Thank You that You are there for me, and You always
understand how I feel and what I struggle with. Amen.

The following morning was an anxious time. Isabel couldn't seem to focus. She kept looking at her phone. Time almost seemed to grind to a standstill. Would the day of dread never end?

Eventually a small car drove into the car park. A tiny runabout. Isabel had expected something bigger, something showier, something to belittle other cars, something that said, 'My dad is rich and bought me this!'

Isabel watched as three young women in their late teens got out. She didn't want revenge or to upstage them in any way. She just wanted the day to be over.

As they walked across the yard towards the office, they looked exceedingly nervous, dressed in jeans, jumpers and trainers. Isabel was surprised how short they looked – she'd always remembered them as being bigger and stronger than her.

Isabel realised that for once she had the upper hand. In the hope of keeping things that way, she advanced towards them, ready to make her introductions. Silently she prayed, 'Hi God, I need Your help now, please.'

She opened her mouth to speak.

'Well, if it isn't little Isabel Price!' Madeleine had always been the ringleader. 'We heard through the grapevine that you were working here. So we thought we'd come and learn to ride.'

The word 'little' echoed in Isabel's mind, but she was determined not to react. Surely they hadn't booked in just to bully her again?

She wasn't going to be put down in her own equestrian centre – or be led into a battle of sarcasm and scorn!

'Madeleine, Rosemary and Heather. How are you all?'

Rosemary smiled. 'I'm good, thank you.'

'I'm a bit nervous,' Heather said, anxiously. 'Horses always seem so big and scary, but I've always wanted to learn to ride.'

Isabel wanted to reply that the three of them had always seemed so big and scary to her at school, but it hadn't worried them. 'Don't worry. We'll take things one stage at a time, to build up your confidence and make you safe riders.'

Madeleine frowned. 'There's nothing to it. Anyone can sit on a horse.'

Isabel was determined that even Madeleine was not going to take away her dignity. 'Your horses are all ready for you. Alec and I will get them out and show you how to get on properly and safely.'

'I know we had a bit of a laugh with you at school – but I hope there are no hard feelings, eh? You were so shy and quiet, and never retaliated. What were we supposed to do?' Madeleine walked towards the horse she would be riding. 'But it's all in the past now, eh?' She glanced over her shoulder.

Isabel had longed to speak to the bullies, tell them about the damage they had done to her through their actions at school. But looking at Madeleine's hard face, she realised that it would serve no useful purpose. 'Let's get you on, guys.'

It wasn't long before Madeleine discovered that horse riding was not as easy as she had imagined, as she really struggled to do rising trot. But Isabel was nothing but encouraging.

Before long, Madeleine had realised that she had to listen carefully to Isabel's instructions – and her respect for her instructor appeared to increase by the minute.

After the lesson, Isabel was quite surprised when Madeleine meekly asked if they could book another lesson at the same time the following week.

Isabel was left with a mixture of feelings about meeting up with the girls again. That evening, as she and Karen sat in the kitchen enjoying a mug of hot chocolate before going to bed – with only the company of Colin – Isabel decided to share some of her feelings with her friend.

'You know those three girls who came for a beginner's lesson today?' Karen nodded. 'Do you know who they were?'

Karen looked confused. 'I can't remember their names, offhand.'

Isabel interrupted. 'I don't mean it like that. I mean, do you know who they were?'

Karen shook her head. 'You're not making any sense.'

'They were the girls who bullied me at school – you know, before I moved to the sixth form college.'

Karen put her mug of hot chocolate down. Eventually she broke the silence. 'I see. Oh, Isabel!'

She got up, put her arms around her friend and gave her a bear hug. And then she sat down again, ready to listen.

The two girls were very late to bed that night, but Isabel felt the satisfaction of having spoken about her ordeal openly, and in detail, for the very first time.

It was sad when, a few days later, they began to pack, ready to move out from the old farmhouse. Of course, they were going to have to vacate the stable yard as well.

'It was a good job you noticed that advert in the local paper yesterday, Karen,' Isabel said, as she carefully wrapped a china horse in bubble wrap. 'At least we've been able to rent a large meadow and two stables, just outside town.'

Karen frowned. 'I don't know how well those stable doors will hold Henry – after all, he is a stallion.'

'We can always strengthen the door a bit,' Ben consoled.

'But at the end of the day, it can only ever be a temporary solution. We need more than two stables for the winter months; we need an office, a tack room and a barn... and most of all, we need a schooling area.' Karen angrily tossed a large blue teapot into a box. Crash! 'I should have done that with a bit more care!'

'At least we've got somewhere to put the horses for the rest of the summer and autumn,' Isabel said.

Fortunately, Ben had a friend with a small industrial unit which he wasn't using currently, and had offered it to them for storage of saddlery, furniture and so on. And they had been able to agree first refusal on a very old residential caravan – at a reasonable price.

That night, when Isabel went up to her room, she did some serious business with God. So much so that she unintentionally found herself praying aloud:

> *Hi God. I really need to talk. I know You always answer prayer, but not always in the way we hope for. Sometimes You say 'no' or 'wait'. And I get that, because You know best. The thing is this: I'm not sure what You're saying to me now – whether You're saying, I'm doing it a different way, no or wait? Well, time is getting a bit short now and we're getting quite anxious about what's going to happen. Please help me to trust You more and to believe that You will sort things out with the centre somehow. Let me be optimistic. And help Karen to believe in the power of prayer.*
> *Can I talk to You again about my relationship with Dad and Mum? Please help us to be close, like we used to be. It would be great if they could be proud of me for who I am and what I'm doing with the horses – and not to keep on about me wasting my dad's money, which he has spent on my education. I think that's going to be an ongoing task!*
> *And then there's dear Aunty Florence. She's still rather feisty at times. Please help her to mellow a bit more. Stan is good for her, because he brings the best out in her. Maybe they will get married, but I leave that to You.*
> *Please help me to always see the best in people.*
> *Amen.*

Isabel heard the floorboards on the landing creek. Had someone been listening to her pray?

Twenty-seven

July

A few days later, Karen organised a spontaneous meeting. Typically of Karen, she had set the kitchen table out with notepads, pens and glasses of water.

'It looks very formal,' Isabel commented as she came in from the yard. 'I hope you haven't invited Crawford-Smith to this one.'

'Definitely not! Just family and work colleagues.'

At that moment, Aunty Florence and Stan hurried in from the hall.

'I hope we're not late,' Stan said apologetically.

'Of course we're not late,' Aunty Florence responded with conviction.

Karen cleared her throat. 'We're just waiting for Ben. He's on his way back from Norwich. I think he's about five minutes away.'

'Let's make some tea, then,' Aunty Florence said, making a beeline for the kettle.

Minutes later, a car pulled into the driveway.

The back door swung open. 'I'm home,' Ben called out to the waiting audience.

Everyone sat down, and Aunty Florence handed round cups of tea.

'What's this all about?' Ben asked.

Isabel nervously started playing with her pen. 'Has something happened?'

There was a moment of silence before Karen replied, 'We're here to talk about future plans.'

'I hope we're included?' Aunty Florence said.

Stan was his ever-genial self. 'It's OK, we understand if you youngsters don't want us oldies getting in the way.'

'Do we?' Aunty Florence turned to him abruptly.

'What are you talking about?' Karen interrupted. 'Of course you're both included. Aunty Florence, you're family, and this is your home. Stan, you're part of everything, you know you are.'

'I would love to stay with you, for the foreseeable future anyway,' Aunty Florence said, 'whether it be here, in a caravan or in new premises.'

Over a second pot of tea, everyone spoke openly about their hopes and dreams for the future of the centre. Karen spoke about her plans for Henry, both as a show jumper and for his next season standing at stud. Stan and Isabel talked about Diana's first expected foal, and their hope of purchasing some additional suitable coloured broodmares. Aunty Florence expressed how pleased she was to have found somewhere where she belonged, at long last – and people who loved her. But, of course, their hopes and dreams all depended on what the next few weeks held in store.

The following week, the expected letter arrived in the morning post from the company they had approached for sponsorship.

Karen clasped the large envelope, obviously nervous about opening it.

'Go on, Karen, open it up and see what they're offering,' Isabel said as she hovered, expectantly.

'They might not be offering us anything,' Karen responded, appearing to be in no hurry to find out.

Stan looked into her face, speaking gently to his young friend. 'After all we have been through over the last few months, the most important thing we've learned is to not give up hope. We are just as deserving as the next stud or equestrian centre. But even if we don't get a deal, we will survive without it.'

'I suppose.' She tentatively tore open the envelope and pulled out the contents. 'They're going to let us have a brand-new horse lorry to carry four horses and with living accommodation!'

'No! Really?' Isabel exclaimed.

'No... No lorry.' Karen threw down the letter in disgust. 'Joking! Seriously now. Not even a dressage saddle or a set of show jumps.'

'What have we got, then?' Isabel asked. 'Is it a cash allowance? Maybe funding for entry fees and travel?'

'No.'

Aunty Florence hurried over and tried to grab the letter. 'Come on, Karen, don't keep us in suspense. What does it say?'

'Wait,' Karen said, frowning as she read the letter again. 'They are giving us one bag of performance cubes.'

There was absolute silence for two or three minutes – broken by a peel of raucous laughter.

'Let's go out and celebrate somewhere tonight,' Isabel suggested.

Everyone was in agreement.

'Why not!' Karen said, ruefully.

Isabel was thrilled when she was given the go-ahead to ride again.

It was a bright summer's day.

'Be careful,' Karen warned as she gave her friend a leg up onto Maria, one of the quieter school horses.

Isabel sat for a moment. It felt wonderful to be on horseback again. She patted the mare gently on the neck before shuffling about in the saddle to get comfortable and into the correct position. 'My joints feel a bit stiff, after not riding for so long.'

'Did you hear what I said?'

'You fuss too much.' Isabel sat up straight, squeezed with her legs and allowed the mare to walk on with her hands and seat. 'This feels so good!'

'Where are you going?' Karen asked.

'I'll just take her into the outdoor school for a half an hour.'

Karen ran to open up the gate.

When Isabel returned to the kitchen for lunch, she was greeted with some bad news.

Karen was holding the local newspaper in her hand. 'I just noticed that Archie has died suddenly – a heart attack. There's an article about him here. Apparently he did a lot of charitable work.'

Isabel looked over her friend's shoulder. There was a large photograph of Archie, standing next to his vintage car.

'He seemed to be a very lonely person,' Isabel commented, 'after he lost his wife.'

Alec walked in, rubbing his hands together. 'Is lunch ready?' he asked.

'Archie has died,' Karen repeated.

Alec looked blank. 'Did I know him?'

At that moment Aunty Florence walked into the kitchen.

'Archie has died,' Karen repeated once again.

'Oh,' Aunty Florence commented. 'That's sad.'

'Hi, Hannah,' Isabel greeted the girl that afternoon. 'It's good of you to come to help us give some of the ponies a good groom. We'll start with Cyril.'

They walked towards the stable together. 'The grooming kit is already up there. I've put a headcollar on Cyril and tied him up ready.'

Hannah was obviously looking round for something, or someone. 'Is Alec about?'

'He's around somewhere, I expect,' Isabel replied, as she opened the stable door. 'Hello, fella.'

Hannah dug into the grooming kit, produced a hoof pick and began to clean out the cob's feet. 'I like Alec; he's kind.'

Isabel nodded, as she got to work with a body brush and curry comb. 'How's school going these days?'

'Not too bad, since Dad spoke to the head teacher,' Hannah replied. 'Summer holidays in a couple of days! That will be good. But I don't know how I would manage if this place wasn't here.'

Isabel stood still for a moment, deep in thought. 'It's really important that we keep going – but God knows that already.'

Half an hour later, Alec popped his head over the stable door. 'Would you like to come and help me to groom Molly, please, Hannah, when you've finished Cyril?'

'I think we've just about finished him now,' Isabel said, as she winked at Hannah, and the girl blushed. 'You can go and help Alec, if you like.'

Hannah hurried off to help Alec with the big Irish draught horse.

Nothing more was said about the sudden passing away of Archie until the phone rang a few days later. Isabel picked it up.

'Hello. Henry's…'

'Could I speak with Miss Isabel Price, please?'

'Speaking.'

'This is Dawson and Son, Solicitors. Mr Dawson Junior speaking.'

'Yes?'

'I am calling about the reading of Mr Archie Johnson's will. It would be good if you could be present at eleven tomorrow morning, at our office in town.'

'What… Why?'

'All will be revealed tomorrow.'

'Oh! OK. I'll be there.'

'What shall I wear?' Isabel asked, the next day.

Aunty Florence had a mischievous twinkle in her eye. 'I could lend you one of my black dresses – then you could look very solemn.'

'Really?'

'She's pulling your leg. Just wear something smart and respectful,' Karen said.

Moments later, Isabel returned with some 'smart' navy blue trousers and a matching top. 'Will this be OK?'

Karen nodded in approval and pointed to the clock on the mantelpiece. 'Shouldn't you be going soon?'

'Is that the time?' Isabel hurried up the stairs to get changed.

Mr Dawson Junior led the way into his office, followed by Isabel and a couple of other people who had obviously also been invited for the reading of Archie's will. 'Please sit down, ladies and gentlemen.'

Isabel thought that Mr Dawson Junior seemed a little too old to be a 'Junior'. The office seemed dark and oppressive – the walls were panelled with some kind of very dark wood and the windows were divided into small panes of glass by strips of lead. She breathed in deeply – the padded dining chairs that they had been invited to sit on smelled fusty. Isabel could feel a tickle in her throat; unwilling to break the silence, she swallowed hard in an effort to restrain the cough reflex.

Moments later, a young woman confidently marched into the room, carrying a file, and handed it to Mr Dawson Junior. He cleared his throat before addressing the gathered audience.

Isabel waited nervously, wondering why she had been chosen to be present. Suddenly the solicitor read out her name. She sat up.

'To Miss Isabel Price I leave my late wife's diamond ring, for her kindness and honesty. Please do with it as you will.'

'But I hardly knew him!' Isabel exclaimed. 'I'm sure I don't deserve it.'

The solicitor handed a small package to his secretary, who passed it on to Isabel.

A woman – Isabel guessed, probably in her fifties – sitting next to her, wearing a black headscarf, reached out and took hold of Isabel's hand. 'Daddy wanted you to have the ring. He thought you could sell it and use the money in your business. He often used to speak about your honesty.'

The solicitor continued to read out Archie's bequests.

Isabel arrived home feeling a mixture of excitement and sadness.

'I feel guilty thinking about selling the ring, but just think what we could do with the money in the business,' Isabel told Karen, Stan and Aunty Florence.

'But I'm sure he left it to you to be sold in order to use the money for the centre – and not to just keep the ring locked away somewhere,' Aunty Florence reasoned.

Isabel nodded. 'His daughter said that he wanted me to sell the ring and use the money for the business. But like Ben said, it isn't enough to help the centre, is it?'

Karen shook her head. 'So, what are you going to spend the money on?'

Isabel's eyes twinkled. 'I'll use some of the money to buy a quality, coloured broodmare. What do you think?'

'Sounds good to me,' Karen smiled. 'Dependent on how God answers your prayers.'

A few days later, Isabel unexpectedly received a letter from France. She recognised the handwriting as her mother's. Isabel carried the letter into the kitchen, where Karen was busy on her laptop, after doing the morning feeds.

'I wonder what my mum wants,' Isabel commented. 'Look at me; I'm trembling.'

Karen shut down her laptop and stood up to put her arm around her friend. 'Hurry up and open it; then you'll find out what she wants.'

Isabel sat down. She was all fingers and thumbs as she struggled to get the contents of the envelope out. 'Look! It's a card, and it's got a picture of a horse on!'

She began to read:

> *Dear Isabel,*
> *I felt that I had to write to you as we couldn't leave things as they were, last time we parted. I don't expect we will be able to put things right overnight. But at least we can try. I am working on your father. It would be good if we could both come over to stay locally for a few days in the not too distant future – but he is going to take a lot of persuading. I will keep in touch.*
> *Love, Mum*

No one spoke for a few moments; even Colin lay quietly in his bed. Tears rolled down Isabel's cheeks as she stood examining the card. She pictured once again those happy days as a small child, when her mother lovingly waved her off to school. She believed that if they all worked on the relationship... well, just maybe!

'There's a lot of healing that needs to take place for those relationships to be restored,' Karen commented.

Isabel nodded. 'As Mum says, we'll have to work at it and see how it goes. But she did sign it, "Love, Mum".'

Colin got up, walked across and rested his chin on Isabel's knee.

'He wants you to be happy,' Karen said, as she smiled. 'We've seen Aunty Florence mellow... surely this long-term feud between you and your parents can be sorted out.'

Isabel wiped her eyes. 'You reckon?'

'I hope so.' Karen hesitated. 'You know what? Maybe these prayers of yours really do work.'

Isabel smiled as she patted Colin on the head. 'Let's go out into the yard and get on.'

As Isabel passed Diana, she grinned as she thought about the foal inside her, and its potential. Then a shiver went down her spine: perhaps it was the chill of the coastal breeze.

She turned towards her friend. 'What if we lose the yard?'

Karen didn't reply.

Isabel looked up and whispered, 'It's all up to You, now, God; we've done all we can.'

Twenty-eight

August

'Are you sure this is the right way to the auction house?' Karen quizzed anxiously.

'Who's driving, you or me?' Ben replied sharply.

'Come on, you guys. Today is going to be hard enough without being at each other's throats,' Isabel remarked.

'There it is, on the right!' Stan pointed towards a car park sign.

Ben braked sharply and swerved into the gateway, causing Aunty Florence to lose her balance and grab hold of Stan's knee for support.

Isabel, crammed in the back of Ben's car with the older couple, laughed. 'What are you two like?'

Just for a moment the atmosphere lightened.

'I hope we can find somewhere to park,' Ben said, as he searched for a free space. 'It looks like the auction will be really busy.'

Suddenly Karen pointed. 'Look, there's Crawford-Smith!'

Isabel was beginning to wish they hadn't come; after all, they'd got no money to buy the centre. The potential £10,000 for the ring was all they had, and that wouldn't be nearly enough for the deposit on an affordable mortgage.

'Nothing short of a miracle can save us now!' Isabel sighed.

Ben turned into a space. 'OK, then. Let's see what happens.'

'We know what will happen,' Karen commented, decisively.

After everyone had got out, Ben locked the doors and they followed the signs to the auction room. There was an aroma of leather, furniture polish and freshly brewed coffee.

'It's very smart,' Karen observed.

'Look at all these people in their best suits,' Isabel whispered. 'They look very rich and powerful.'

'Yes, and they're destroying small businesses,' Karen said out loud.

'Shhh!' Isabel told her. 'Someone might hear.'

'I don't care if they do.'

'But we can't tar all these people with the same brush as Crawford-Smith – it wouldn't be fair.'

Aunty Florence gently put her hand on her niece's arm. 'Don't upset yourself, dear.'

At that moment, Stan darted off towards the front.

'Where's Stan gone rushing off to?' Isabel asked.

Aunty Florence turned round in surprise, 'What? Oh, I expect he's gone to the toilet before the auction starts.'

'There's a lot of people if that's a queue for the toilet!'

It seemed to be ages before Stan returned. As he did, a rather smartly dressed gentleman came into the hall through a door at the side of the small platform, complete with clipboard and gavel. He settled at a large oak lectern and called everyone to order. Immediately the audience settled down, obviously afraid that they could inadvertently buy something with a careless nod or wave.

It seemed a long time before it was the turn of Henry's Stud and Equestrian Centre, together with the old farmhouse. After a brief introduction, the auctioneer opened it up to the floor – the last property of the day.

'What am I bid for this desirable property with development potential? Who will give me £800,000?'

Karen mouthed to Isabel, '£800,000!'

After a moment's hesitation, a man of about forty, at the back in a pinstriped suit, put his hand up.

'Will anyone give me £810,000?'

Immediately, a slim, grey-haired woman on the third row back nodded her head. Within minutes the price was up to £910,000. And five different people were bidding for it: Crawford-Smith, the man in the pinstriped suit, the woman from the third row, a mystery telephone bidder and a nervous young man on the front row who appeared to be bidding on behalf of a client.

'Will anyone give me £920,000?' The auctioneer looked in Crawford-Smith's direction.

To Isabel's surprise he shook his head and walked off out of the hall, fuming, 'Daylight robbery! It's not worth all that!'

'He's dropped out,' Isabel said in a loud whisper. 'Who'd have believed it?'

'But it's not going to do us any good, is it?' Karen said, rather sharply.

The young man on the front row glanced nervously around.

'The bid is with you, madam, on the third row,' the auctioneer announced, obviously ready to draw the bidding to a close.

Suddenly the young man jumped up out of his seat, waving his hands up in the air. '£925,000.'

The auctioneer looked a little surprised. 'The bid is with the gentleman at the front.' As he looked round, the other bidders were shaking their heads. 'Going once, going twice… Sold to the gentleman at the front.'

'Well, that's that!' Karen sighed. 'Let's go back and finish packing our bags.'

The party from the equestrian centre stood up and began to make their way towards the back of the hall. Just as they were going out of the door, someone called Stan's name. He didn't seem to hear.

Isabel touched Stan's arm. 'Someone's calling you.'

'What?' Stan looked surprised.

Isabel pointed towards the front of the hall. 'Oh! I don't believe it. It looks like Roy's son! I remember him from the funeral. What's he doing here? Looks like he wants to speak to you.'

'Oh – so it is. I wonder what he wants. I thought we'd said all that needed to be said.'

'When did you speak to him?' Aunty Florence questioned.

But before Stan had a chance to say anything, Isabel butted in. 'He's coming over.'

'Stan! I'm so glad I caught you. Can we go and have a cup of tea somewhere? I need to talk to you.'

Stan indicated towards the rest of his party. 'We're together.'

'Of course – I believe it's all of you that I need to speak with.'

'What do you think this is all about?' Isabel whispered to Karen.

Karen put her hand in front of her mouth as she replied. 'I hope it's not going to take too long, we've still got packing to be done.'

Aunty Florence surprised everyone by saying, in a loud voice, 'Well, after the stress of the auction, I'm certainly ready for a hot drink!'

It wasn't long before they found a tea shop – a whitewashed cottage with low beams and an inviting smell of freshly brewed coffee. The manager hurried across to the window to push two small tables together to make room for six. Aunty Florence pointed to some floral china plates adorning a high shelf. Stan acknowledged them with a grin, before sitting down. 'It's nice to get the weight off my feet.'

'Tea or coffee?' Roy's son got up and went to the counter. 'Six teas, and some nice cakes please – this is a celebration.' He handed over three £10 notes. 'Keep the change.' He sat down again, squeezing between Aunty Florence and Stan.

'What's this all about, then?' Stan asked at last.

Roy's son smiled. 'Well, it's like this. I've just bought your farmhouse, stable yard and meadows as an investment property. I don't want to redevelop it. And I don't want to run it, because I don't know the first thing about horses. I just wondered if you knew of anyone who would like to rent it from me.'

'What?' Isabel replied excitedly. 'But you weren't even bidding for it.'

He smiled again. 'I never bid myself – I'm too well known – people deliberately bump the price up. The young fellow at the front was one of my employees. He was a little nervous today. It was his first time.'

Isabel was curious. 'But how did you know it was our property, anyway?'

'Stan came over for a chat before the auction.' He smiled. 'And I casually asked what had brought him here.'

Stan looked solemn. 'You did this on purpose, didn't you? You realise that we can't accept. I told you that I didn't want or expect any repayment for what I did for your dad.'

When the tea and cakes arrived, somehow the little group didn't feel like celebrating. Roy's son took a large gulp of tea. 'Look, I buy property. Some of it I redevelop and some I buy to rent out – because property and land is a good long-term investment. I came here to invest some money on a property to rent out. The one I was particularly interested in fetched too much money. Your place seemed like a good, trouble-free investment – valuable buildings and land, tenants already in and running a business – an ideal opportunity to secure a good market rent. Don't let me down, please.'

'I don't believe you,' Stan said wryly.

'Stan! For goodness' sake!' Aunty Florence exclaimed.

'OK, OK. As long as it is a market rent – no favours.'

Karen was quick to confirm, 'We accept your offer. Thank you.'

'I'll get my solicitor to draw up a lease as soon as possible. Now, please eat some of these cakes. We're celebrating, aren't we?'

'Yes,' Ben said, shaking his hand. 'We certainly are.'

Karen wiped her eyes, Aunty Florence hugged Stan, and Isabel breathed a sigh of relief. Between them they'd won the battle. God had won the victory for them – and beaten the bullies. 'Oh, thank You, God. We can go home and start unpacking now,' she said exuberantly.

When they arrived home, Isabel wandered out to the meadow and called Diana over.

'Guess what… we're staying! Henry's Stud and Equestrian Centre is safe – at least for the time being.'

Karen came over to join her friend. 'The battle has been won. The ruthless bullies have been defeated. Roy's son has saved the day.'

'And Diana is in foal,' Isabel added. 'A fresh and exciting new start!'

Karen leaned on the gate and stared into the meadow, 'Your prayers were answered, then.'

'Yes. God answers prayer, but not always in the way we expect – or with a "no" or a "wait". I think God must have been saying "wait" to us! I've still got a long way to go in dealing with my parents – and with completely forgiving the bullies from school.'

'We can begin to look forward to some of our hopes and dreams coming to fruition now,' Karen pointed out.

'Things might not be plain sailing, and there might be more bullies, but we can overcome them, with God's help.'

'You're right.' Karen gave her friend a hug. 'I'm going in to do some unpacking now. Are you coming?'

'I'll be over in a few minutes. I just need to have a quick chat with God to say thank You!'

'Well,' Karen glanced at her as she began to walk away, 'say thanks from me too. OK?'

'I will!' Isabel rubbed her horse fondly on her nose. 'I'll catch up with you later.'